Gone Crazy in Alabama

Gone Crazy in Alabama

by Rita Williams-Garcia

Amistad

An Imprint of HarperCollins*Publishers*

Amistad is an imprint of HarperCollins Publishers.

Gone Crazy in Alabama
Copyright © 2015 by Rita Williams-Garcia
All rights reserved. Printed in the United States of America.
No part of this book may be used or reproduced in any manner whatsoever
without written permission except in the case of brief quotations embodied
in critical articles and reviews. For information address HarperCollins
Children's Books, a division of HarperCollins Publishers, 195 Broadway,
New York, NY 10007.
www.harpercollinschildrens.com

Library of Congress Control Number: 2014922274
ISBN 978-0-06-221587-1 (trade bdg.)
ISBN 978-0-06-221588-8 (lib. bdg.)

Typography by Laura DiSiena
15 16 17 18 19   CG/RRDH   10 9 8 7 6 5 4 3 2 1

First Edition

For the memories of Mary Edwards Coston
and Edith King Lloyd Williams, my grandmothers

Contents

It Takes a Licking

Vonetta, Fern, and I didn't sleep well last night or the night before. There's something about preparing for a trip that draws my sisters and me closer together than we already are. Maybe it's the planning and excitement of going places or seeing who we're going to see.

As soon as we dragged our suitcases out of the attic, my sisters and I race-walked along Herkimer Street and headed to Mr. Mack's store on Fulton to buy a bag of candy that would last the whole trip down south. We planned to fill our hands with different-flavored Jolly Rancher sucking candy, wax lips, and Pixy Stix, plus Bazooka bubble gum to last the whole trip, starting from Brooklyn, New York, then to New Jersey, all the way down to Georgia and lastly to Alabama. Vonetta was good at keeping track of things and divvying them up between us, so I let her be in charge of handing out the "new state" candy. Candy was enough to send Vonetta and Fern over the moon, but it didn't mean the same thing to me. It was too hot for Mr. Goodbar, and a box of Good & Plenty only reminded me of watching movies at the RKO with my pa. All of that was different now that I shared him with Mrs., but as long as Pa's wife stayed with us in our house on Herkimer Street, even after their fights, I gladly shared my father.

We were about to go inside Mr. Mack's when three girls who had been in Vonetta's third-grade class two years ago came out laughing and chewing on long red licorice. "Hi, Vonetta!" they all sang at her.

"Hi," Vonetta returned weakly.

"Hi!" Fern echoed, but louder.

Then they sashayed past us, the one wearing Vonetta's watch snaking her wrist around and around like a baton twirler, except there was no baton. Just Vonetta's watch. The watch Vonetta had let her "hold" and never got back. She sashayed and twirled her wrist and arm purposely so Vonetta could see her watch, and when Vonetta did nothing and said nothing, I got angry. At her.

I said, "Vonetta, go get your watch."

Vonetta tried to act like she didn't hear me but I knew she did.

"Don't think I'm going to get it for you."

2

"No one asked you to." She tried to sound tough, like she wasn't afraid of me. "Besides, I didn't want that old watch in the first place."

"Yeah," Fern said. "She wanted a charm bracelet. With ballet slippers, a heart, and a shamrock for luck."

"Not a stupid watch," Vonetta said. "All it can do is tell time."

"Tell time, take a licking, and keep on ticking," Fern sang.

Vonetta sucked her teeth. "Licking and ticking. What's so special about that?"

I said, "Pa gave it to you. That's what's special about your watch."

"So." She rolled huge cow eyes at me. I didn't care what our mother, Cecile, had told me about looking after Vonetta. I wanted to knock her out.

Then Fern said, "Yeah. So. If it's so special, and she should have it, where's *my* watch?"

Fern planted both hands on her nothing hips and tapped her toe, doing her best Vonetta impression. Turning eight hadn't grown Fern any taller. It had just made her mouthy.

"Where's *my* watch?" she repeated.

"Safe in my drawer, where you won't lose it."

"Well, I want it," Fern said. "And you can't keep it from me. If you don't cough it up, I'll tell Mrs."

I shrugged. "Tell Mrs."

3

"I'll tell her and she'll tell you—"

Then Vonetta, her ally, cleared her throat, fluttered her eyelashes, and finished in a voice as close to our step-mother's as she could mimic, "Delphine. Your sister is capable of wearing a watch." *Capable* was one of Mrs.'s words. She used it against me to make me stop helping my sisters. *Vonetta is capable of doing her own hair.* Then Vonetta burned her ears with the hot comb, and who had to rub Vaseline on burned ears and finish pulling the hot comb through Vonetta's thick, thick head? Not Mrs.

"Fine," I told them both. "And when you lose your watch, don't come crying to me."

"Boo, hoo, hoo," Fern said. "Delphine, you better gimme my watch when we get home."

We left the house giddy and returned crabby. A giant sack of candy made no difference.

I had chicken to wash, flour, and fry and a lemon cake to bake and frost. It all had to be done before I went to bed that night. Pa said we had to be up before the sun to get the first Greyhound down to Atlanta. From there, Big Ma and her neighbor, Mr. Lucas, would be waiting to drive us over the state line to Alabama to our great-grandmother's little yellow house that sat just on the edge of Prattville on twenty acres that ended at a creek.

Mrs. poked her Afro into the kitchen to offer her help but she looked as green as she had earlier that morning. Pa

4

said it was the summertime flu but I knew better. There's no monthlong flu, summer, winter, or otherwise. I said, "No, thank you. I'm almost done." Mrs. seemed grateful and went back to the sofa to lie down.

I preferred my sisters' company in the kitchen but we weren't exactly on speaking terms, which was hard to maintain because our voices either followed or lay on top of one another's for as long as I could remember. We spoke almost like one person, one voice, but each of us saying our own part, kind of like those records Cecile used to play with a singer's voice catting and scatting like a horn, piano, and bass. Or like Pa's old doo-wop records with duos and trios that went high, higher, then low. We've been laying our voices down, catting and scatting, and following variations of the same notes for so long we didn't always know we were doing it. But others noticed. The way we flowed in and out of our words drove Mrs. crazy, and she'd give us the eye like, *Cut it out.* "You're individuals," she'd say. "One complete thought for each complete person." But when you're used to speaking as one, it's hard to stop just because someone is under your roof and says stop.

As I whipped, beat, and stirred the lemon cake batter, I missed hearing my sisters' voices and having them around me.

Vonetta, Fern, and I could afford to have our little scraps. Closing a door behind us and stomping away didn't mean a thing. Sooner or later Vonetta or Fern would open the door to my room or I'd open the door to theirs. My sisters and I might quarrel but we didn't stay mad or gone too long a period from one another's sight.

Heaven knows we've had our share of long gone. Like our uncle Darnell, who'd left us after he had stolen from my sisters and me. I knew it was his fighting in Vietnam that made him turn to drugs, and I knew it was the drugs that made him steal from us. I didn't know how much I'd miss him when he left.

It seems every time the door to our house on Herkimer Street is slammed shut too hard, pictures flash before me. Pictures of Cecile, our mother, leaving back when my sisters were barely walking and I was four years old.

I've been dreaming a lot lately, kicking the covers every which way. I've been dreaming . . . running to the door to keep it from closing hard . . . to keep footsteps from walking out . . . walking away . . . away . . . But as long as my legs are, I never get to the front door fast enough. As strong as my arms are, I can't keep Cecile from leaving. Uncle Darnell from leaving. Big Ma from leaving. Or Mrs., when she's mad . . .

I can't stop the dreams. I can't stop seeing the opened door and the footsteps.

Things Fell Apart

The next morning Pa gathered us around for what was usually a Pa and Delphine talk. The talk where he told me everything I needed to know to get my sisters and me safely to our destination. This time Vonetta and Fern were also under his chin as he spoke.

"I don't want to hear about you two acting up on the ride down." Vonetta and Fern gave him cow-eyed innocence but Pa smiled, knowing better. "Delphine, I don't like putting this on you, but if anyone asks, you're thirteen."

"But twelve rides cheaper, Pa," I said. I only had a few months before I became an official teenager. I could wait, but I didn't want to admit that to my father.

"Can I be eleven?" Vonetta asked.

Pa said, "Ten's good enough for you."

"And eight's great." Fern found her spot and jumped in. She rhymed and played with her words like she played with peas, butterbeans, and mashed potatoes at the table. It was those poetry letters to and from Cecile that got her playing with words at every opportunity.

I sang, "I'll bet we'll save a few dollars if I ride as my real age."

Mrs. picked up the tune. "Did someone say save a few dollars?" It was good to hear Mrs. joke for a change. She smiled but her skin looked dull and greenish.

"Good one, Marva," Pa said. "But we don't need the whole world worrying about kids riding on a bus without an adult."

Mrs. had been lying on the couch and propped herself up. "Louis, honey. Maybe we should—"

But Pa put his hand up, and to my surprise, Mrs., an out-and-out women's libber, closed her mouth and lay her head back down on the sofa pillow. Mrs. smiled, but I could see how tired she was and that her eyes were losing their sassy spark. I hated to see Mrs. change. It had taken a while, but I had gotten used to her beaming and grinning at Pa, calling him "old-fashioned" and "country." I had gotten used to Mrs. talking her women's-lib talk. It was funny how Big Ma had always warned Pa that Mrs. would upset the household. As I watched her grow quiet, tired, and nauseous, I knew it was the other way around: Pa was

8

changing Mrs. before Mrs. could upset the house.

"There'll be a bunch of kids going down south to spend the summer with folks. A few parents on the bus to keep an eye on things. They'll be fine," Pa said.

"Honey, don't you think—"

"Sweetie, you worry too much, and you know that's not good for you," Pa said. He pointed his finger at Vonetta and Fern. "I mean what I say: I don't want to hear about you two causing a stir, having the world looking at three colored girls, wondering where their father and mother are."

"They won't," I said.

Then Vonetta said, "We won't," raising her voice over mine. "We know how to act on a bus trip."

"And we act splendidly on a plane," Fern said. "Splendidly and perfectly."

They both said together, "Or on a train."

Vonetta punched Fern in the shoulder first. "Jinx!"

Pa shook his head. "That's what I mean. None of that bickering and hitting. One minute you're play-fighting. The next minute you're cats in the alley. You can't have any of that on the bus."

"We won't," they chimed. Chimed and lied.

"Well, I better not hear about it," Pa said. "I better not get a call from the state police."

"You won't, Papa." More chiming and lying.

"I mean it. You two, mind your sister. You hear?"

"We will." Their notes were high, sweet, and fake.

Even Pa shook his head.

Instead of driving the Buick Wildcat from Brooklyn to the Port Authority in Manhattan, Pa drove us down to Newark, New Jersey, to catch the Greyhound. He said it was to save a few dollars but I knew better. If Pa wanted to save money, I wouldn't be traveling down south as a thirteen-year-old adult. I'd pay the children's fare like my sisters, and Pa would have told one of the bus-riding mothers to keep an eye on his little girls. Pa's first thought wasn't to save money. He drove us to Newark because he wanted to spend time with us. Just us.

"Mind yourselves down there," Pa said. Even though we'd been south visiting Big Ma and her mother, Ma Charles, when we were younger, Pa felt the need to remind us, "The South's not like Bed-Stuyvesant and you can't get more southern than Alabama." To Vonetta, he said, "Don't go grinning at every white kid trying to make friends. Stick to your own and you won't have any problems. If they call you a name, keep your mouth shut and walk away." Then to Fern, he said, "Don't ball up your fists at everyone who says something you don't like."

"We can handle white kids," I said. "We can handle racist names."

"And racist oppressors."

10

"Trying to keep the black man down."

Pa shook his head. "That's exactly what I mean." He looked to the sky. "Why did I send you girls to Oakland?"

"So we could be strong black girls," I answered, although the real answer was so we could see our mother.

"Black and proud."

"Black and loud."

"Power to the people."

"None of that while you're down there. Delphine, this is no joke. None of that black power stuff in Alabama. Black Panthers strut about in Brooklyn and in Oakland, but they're not so loud and proud in Alabama and Mississippi. Once you cross the line from North to South all of that black power stuff is over."

"So we better get it all out now!" I said. My sisters and I started chanting, "Ungawa, Ungawa. Soul is black power." Then, "Free Huey, seize the time!" and every other Black Panther slogan we learned last summer in Oakland with Cecile and the Black Panthers.

Pa let us get it all out of our systems and then he said, "You had your fun. I need you to listen. Really listen."

"Yes, Papa," I said, taking the silliness out of my voice.

"The South isn't like Brooklyn. You're not freedom riders going down south to kick up some dust. You girls have some mouths on you; I don't know who to blame for that—your mother, Marva, or those Panthers. I want you to stay together. Don't let one separate from the other. I'm

11

counting on you, Delphine. Keep your sisters in line and together."

Pa sounded like his mother, Big Ma, worrying about white people. But Pa's voice was steady and firm and his eyebrows pinched together. He meant for us to hear his every word. Our grandmother used to fuss with us so much that all we heard was the fussing and not the words. That was when Big Ma lived with us in Brooklyn on Herkimer Street. But then Pa married Miss Marva Hendrix and Uncle Darnell left us and Big Ma got on a Greyhound and returned to her house in Alabama. Like the title of my sixth-grade teacher's favorite book, things at our house in Herkimer Street fell apart.

On the Road

The bus was like Pa said it would be. More kids traveling down south than adults. Half of the travelers wore blue and white T-shirts that declared them Young Saints of Shiloh Baptist from Queens. Ours was a double-decker bus, which was exciting in itself. We had never been on a double-decker bus and we all said, "I want to go up there!" The bus driver, a man older than our father but not as old as Big Ma, stopped us. "Bunch of teenagers up there. Young ones stay where I can see you. Plenty of seats down here."

I started to tell the driver I was thirteen and could watch my sisters, but Vonetta told him, "You can't drive the bus *and* keep an eye on us," and then I said, "Shut

13

your mouth, Vonetta," and as if Big Ma had been poking me in the back telling me what to say, I added, "Sorry, sir," and we moved down the narrow aisle to join the Young Saints.

My sisters sat together on one side of the aisle and I sat across from them in the aisle seat, next to a boy about my age. I geared myself up for some conversation, mainly to practice talking to a real teenage boy, but he closed his eyes almost as soon as I slid into the seat next to him. That was fine with me, although some conversation would have been nice. Besides, I would get in all the practice I wanted in talking to teenage boys when we got to my great-grandmother Ma Charles's house. My cousin JimmyTrotter would do. And I hoped he felt like talking. I hoped he wasn't sad and quiet like he was when we left Alabama three years ago. But I'd understand if he was.

The plan to dole out one piece of bubble gum, one Jolly Rancher sucking candy, and a Pixy Stix for every state we entered fell apart long before we reached the middle of Virginia, but that was all right. I glanced over at my sisters. Vonetta erased and filled in her crossword puzzle. Fern read *Charlotte's Web*. I didn't know how much longer they'd remain fuss-free but I was grateful for their good behavior and plowed onward with *Things Fall Apart*.

I'd been saving my book since Christmas, waiting for a long stretch of time that didn't include bickering sisters, a heap of chores, and homework. When Pa announced our bus trip I knew I'd have hours and hours on the road with the perfect companion if my sisters let me read in peace. I felt a surge of pride as I read my first adult book—and a book about Africa written by an African. With everyone in the neighborhood taking on African names and trying to go back to Africa, I was anxious to learn more about the place of our ancestors.

It didn't take too long for me to know I wouldn't be changing my name to some Swahili translation for "oldest, tallest daughter." Even the cherry Jolly Rancher soured in my mouth as I read. How could this be a great African novel if the people weren't so great?

The more I read, the less I liked Okonkwo, the main character. I couldn't understand why the writer would spend an entire book on such a mean, selfish ogre, or why my sixth-grade teacher thought it was a great book. He'd read the cover ragged! I kept waiting for the story to be the fine literature that even my stepmother declared it to be. Even if Okonkwo changed or did something right or heroic, I still wouldn't like him.

I could have kicked myself for being trapped with mean, murdering Okonkwo when *The Soul Brothers and Sister Lou* and *The Outsiders* rattled around unread in the underbelly of our Greyhound. It wasn't fair to have waited for so long to read a book that was less than what I'd imagined.

15

There I was, without the book I'd hoped for. Stuck for hours and hours with a story I didn't want to read. Next to a boy who wouldn't let me practice boy-talking with him. I might as well have been stuck between Vonetta and Fern, kicking, punching, and yowling like cats.

At least my sisters weren't miserable.

I glanced over at Fern and envied the way she raised her eyebrows, a sure sign that she was loving her story and couldn't wait to turn the page. I could even guess which part of her story she was at. How I longed for any one of my books locked in my suitcase.

When we pulled in for our stop in Spartanburg, South Carolina, the bus driver refused to let me retrieve my other books from my suitcase, no matter how politely I asked. *You think I can haul out every piece of luggage for every passenger?* The bus driver didn't have time for that, although he did retrieve my seatmate's luggage—only because Spartanburg turned out to be the boy's stop. We didn't even bother to say any good-byes, and to boot, I'd soon be stuck with mean and unlucky Okonkwo for the rest of our trip, and we had a long, long way to go.

My sisters and I stood guard for one another in the bathrooms at every rest stop. If we stopped long enough, we'd join a few of the Young Saints from the bus for games of freeze tag and Mother May I? until it was time to reboard the bus. I didn't want to use up our money in

Spartanburg, but I had to reload our cooler with snacks and drinks for the rest of the ride.

There were only two working telephone booths. I was overdue for the call home to let Pa and Mrs. know that we were safely on our journey. I was anxious to get to the phone booth and had to wait my turn. I took my dimes and quarters and fed them into the slot, each coin clinking down one after the other. I dialed the number while Vonetta and Fern cupped their hands at the coin return just in case. I had everything well timed. The phone rang once. I prepared to hang up the receiver but I heard a sound on the other end. *A voice.* It was Mrs. She'd picked up the phone when she was supposed to let it ring. Now we'd lose our coins!

"Hullo?" Her voice was heavy with sleep.

It was too late to hang up so I answered. "Hello, Mrs."

"Delphine!" She perked up like she missed us and was genuinely glad to hear my voice. I couldn't stop Vonetta and Fern from saying their hellos in the background, and she seemed to like it because she laughed.

"We're fine, Mrs. But you weren't supposed to pick up the phone," I said, almost scolding her. "Pa and I had it worked out so I could call in one more time before we got to Atlanta."

"Pure nonsense!" Mrs. declared. "Pure, utter nonsense. You call collect at every stop to let us know you and your sisters are all right. I wasn't crazy about you girls traveling south all alone to begin with."

"We're all right," I said.

"We're safe," Vonetta said. "There's lots of kids going south for the summer."

"Surely are. Like birds flying south in the winter."

Then Vonetta made fun of what Fern said and I had to push them away from the phone.

"We're all right," I said again. The last thing I wanted was for Mrs. and Pa to fight over us traveling by ourselves.

"Delphine, you call collect every chance you get," Mrs. said.

"Pa won't like it," I said.

She laughed. "Don't you worry about that."

"Mrs. . . . ?" I asked slowly, even though I was eating up the coins and minutes.

"Yes, Delphine?"

"Is everything with you and Pa—"

She cut me off as if she knew what was on my mind. "Everything is fine, Delphine."

The last fight they had was because Mrs. was sick. Pa said, "I never knew a woman could get so sick," and Mrs. yelled at him, "Stop comparing me to Cecile!" and she took some things and left for a few days. Then she came back.

"And are you—"

"Delphine, I'm fine." I could almost see her smile. "Now stop worrying, and have some fun. It's summertime."

But I couldn't help it. I added, "See you when we get back home," just to hear what she'd say.

"We'll be here," she sang.

She almost sounded like the old Mrs., or like Miss Marva Hendrix. Sure of herself and speaking her mind. It had taken me a while to like her, and I knew I really liked her when I began to miss hearing her speak her mind.

"Fifty cents, please," the operator interrupted. "Please deposit another fifty cents for the next three minutes."

Vonetta and Fern yelped their good-byes and we lost the connection.

Everything Is Everything

No one was happier than Vonetta and Fern to get off the bus for good. We weren't done traveling but at least we'd be off the Greyhound. Now that we'd been cooped up on the bus for more than a day, and Vonetta and Fern had long ago worn out their "best behavior," I saw that Papa knew best by putting us on the bus in New Jersey instead of in New York City. We couldn't have made it one mile farther. Even though the bus transfer from Atlanta to Montgomery would have taken only a few hours, that would have meant a few hours more than we could have stood. It was a miracle Vonetta made it from New Jersey to Atlanta without picking on Fern, and a bigger miracle that Fern's watch still hung from her puny wrist. I was just glad we survived more than a day's worth of riding without a real reason to call home.

Mrs. turned out to be right after all. Pa didn't mind me calling collect when we reached Atlanta. He told me what a good job I had done getting my sisters down south safely and I soaked it in. Neither Pa nor my real mother, Cecile, were long on praise. I had to enjoy the few words they sprinkled when I got them.

Pa said, "You know Mr. Lucas's truck when you see it."

"Yes, Pa," I said. "I know Mr. Lucas's truck when I see it," I repeated back for my sisters.

"I know Mr. Lucas's truck too," Vonetta said.

"It's blue, Papa!" Fern added. "Blue and rusty." I waved my hand to shush them. Still, I couldn't believe Fern remembered the old blue truck. Fern was five when we had come down for the funerals. She was smaller than small and sat on my lap back then.

Fern and Vonetta played invisible hopscotch next to the luggage while I waited for Big Ma and Mr. Lucas to drive up in his truck. Mr. Lucas, a widower with no kids, was practically Big Ma's brother. The Charles and Lucas homes had been standing within shouting distance from each other for more than ninety years. Mr. Lucas had always treated Big Ma's mother, Ma Charles, like she was his mother, and took care of things for our great-grandmother, especially when Big Ma had come to stay with us in Brooklyn.

We still had to drive to Big Ma's small yellow house

that stood on about an acre of land, just off the edge of Prattville proper in Autauga County. I looked forward to seeing the big blue truck. Mr. Lucas was sure to bring us bags of unshelled pecans covered in sugar and salt, and maybe a few ripe peaches. Mr. Lucas and Papa always sang "Old Man River" and other songs on the porch in the evening. Mr. Lucas could dip his voice low to sing baritone and make us laugh. We welcomed his treats and attention. He was the closest thing to a grandpa we'd ever have. We didn't know Cecile's people, and Grandpa Gaither died the year Uncle Darnell was born, although Big Ma never talked about that.

I was the first to see the old Ford truck riding up. Then Vonetta and Fern saw it and stopped in the middle of Fern's hopscotch turn. They began to do their praise dancing, glad that we'd soon see Big Ma and Ma Charles. If Big Ma could have seen them jumping and shouting "Hallelujah!" she would have given them a real reason to jump. But she would have gotten to me first for letting them carry on in public.

The old truck bounced in the distance. When it was maybe one hundred feet away, approaching slowly, I realized Mr. Lucas wasn't behind the wheel. The girls must have realized it also because they stopped praise dancing—Fern reacting to Vonetta, whose face stiffened with recognition.

The truck came to an abrupt halt and lurched forward

all at once. Uncle Darnell got out of the truck and came around. He stood with both hands on his hips and waited. He looked down before he looked up but then he came toward us. I knew Vonetta was still angry over what he had done to us but I missed him, maybe even more than when he'd been fighting in Vietnam. I knew he'd made us cry, and made Big Ma cry and worry, and made Pa hate him. But he was my uncle and I had given up hurting from what he had done to us a long time ago. He was my uncle and I couldn't stop running until I was hugging him.

Vonetta's hurt hadn't dried up and she hadn't forgotten a thing. She couldn't let go because she didn't get it. She couldn't see how our family was scattering, piece by piece. She only cared that Uncle Darnell had stolen our concert money last year and ruined our chance to see the Jackson Five at Madison Square Garden. It didn't matter to her that our uncle had gone to the army hospital to get himself cleaned up and off drugs. You'd have thought she was Fern when she set eyes on Uncle Darnell, clenching her fists and banging them at her sides, ready to fight. Vonetta marched up to Uncle Darnell, took one of her fists, and reared back the way the puncher shouldn't if she didn't want to be the "punchee." Then she gave a war cry before letting him have it in the gut. She had been saving that up for months.

I knew a look of pity and shame when I saw one. He took her punch and said gently, "Vonetta."

"I hate you. You junkie. You thief."

Fern gasped aloud. Her natural instinct was to follow Vonetta, but this time she wouldn't. She loved Michael Jackson, but she loved Uncle D more, and she clamped herself around him in a hug.

That left Vonetta outside of our hug and she seemed happy to not be a part of us.

"You hate me?" Uncle D asked her. "Still?" After all, he had sent us the Jackson Five album by special delivery to make up for stealing from us.

Vonetta showed her teeth like an animal. "I hate you." She breathed short and heavy. "I hate you."

"So you're not going to ride with me up front?" he asked.

Vonetta crossed her arms. "Not for a sack full of candy."

Fern looked at her like she was crazy.

"I'll ride in the back," Vonetta said.

"Ooh! In the truck part, where it's nice and bumpity-bumpy! Me too!" Fern cried.

"There's a huge bag of chicken feed back there to rest against," Uncle D said.

"So," Vonetta said. She hadn't uncrossed her arms.

"Wait." If Uncle Darnell was hurt by Vonetta he didn't show it. He lifted our luggage onto the truck bed, then took a blanket from the front seat, shook it, and spread it down next to the luggage. He lifted Fern up and into the truck. He went to lift Vonetta but she said, "I can climb.

I don't need your help." But she couldn't climb and Uncle heaved her up into the truck bed next to Fern.

"No standing, no horsing around." His voice changed. He was serious.

"We can wave at all the people we pass, right, Uncle Darnell?"

"You bet." I think he waited for Vonetta to add her two cents, the way she normally would if Fern beat her to the first line. Vonetta stayed mum, arms crossed, chin pressed to her chest.

He and I got into the cab and we were off.

Uncle D was different. Older. He wasn't twenty-one yet, but he wasn't the way he used to be. Singing, dancing, telling us stories about princesses in the tower or about the Arabian Knight of Herkimer Street. The war had made him older. And the drugs. I didn't know if people could be fixed. The way they showed it in health films, commercials, and episodes on crime stories, drugs turned you into something or someone else. Like in *Old Yeller*. Old Yeller was a good family dog who got bit by a rabid wolf while protecting the family. Then he became a mad dog foaming at the mouth and the only thing left to do was to shoot him. When Uncle D came home from Vietnam, he became like a ghost rattling his chain and moaning in the night. Then Pa said he had to leave our house.

I glanced at my uncle, who knew I was staring at him. Knew it but kept his eyes straight on the road.

"Uncle D . . ."

"Ask me what you want to ask."

"You're a grown man, right?"

"Grown enough." He squinted against the sun and tilted his head my way. "Go ahead, Delphine. Ask."

"Are you . . . all right?"

He knew what I was asking. Were the drugs gone for good? Did he sleep and moan all the time? Did his sniffling cold go away? And the hollering out in the night. Was that gone too?

"Mostly."

"Mostly?"

Mostly wasn't enough for me or what I wanted to hear. He said, "I did a lot of healing in the army hospital, Delphine. Some on the way down here."

"But you're better, right?"

His eyes went from the road to me and back to the road. Even though I loved him, I had been hurt by him. Underneath it all I was unsure and Fern was probably a little frightened. But only Vonetta was mad enough to stay mad. I asked him again if he was better. I had to tell my sisters to not be afraid and to not be mad. I had to tell them that it was all right. That he was all right.

"Mostly." His voice was flat and old. Like Pa's. "That's all I can give you."

We drove for a little less than three hours. I dozed off, but for how long, I didn't know. When I awoke, the Georgia pine trees had become Alabama pine trees. I knew we were getting closer as every other town name had *creek* in it. We passed this creek town only to enter that creek town. The memories of driving past trees, ponds, lakes, creeks, and rivers flooded back to me from the last time we had driven down three years ago. Ponds and lakes were in Georgia. Rivers and creeks in Alabama. What did it matter? We were far from Brooklyn.

Then Uncle Darnell began to sing Stevie Wonder's "Uptight (Everything's Alright)" but he jumbled the words and sang "Everything is everything." That was how I knew my old Uncle D was still in there.

Moon House

Can a bloodhound remember you from years back and smell you coming from half a mile away? Caleb's welcome grew louder as we drove along the sparsely tree-lined road that would bring us to Ma Charles's property. Uncle D winked at me as if to say, *Girl, you were surely missed,* and my heart clanged worse than when I got my first kiss from Ellis Carter. I wanted to be with my grandmother and my great-grandmother more than anything. I wanted us to all be together. As many of us under one roof as could fit. I needed to know we weren't all falling apart.

I could see Ma Charles's yellow aluminum siding house as we wound around the road. It seemed to have grown larger, and not only as we neared it: its size appeared to have doubled. The girls must have seen the house as well. They sang at the top of their lungs, "I'm Going Back to Indiana" even though we were in the heart of Alabama. I sang along with them. Finally, in the seconds that seemed longest, the truck bounced, shimmied, and slowly trailed up the dirt and gravel driveway of our great-grandmother's house. Even the hens, fenced in by the wire chicken run, clucked and fussed in our honor. Their fussing and squawking went on for as long as it took one hen to spot something tasty on the ground and the others to join in the scuffle to get a piece of it.

Caleb, sturdier than when I saw him last, didn't stop singing his dog song, which was neither a true howl nor a bark. Then Big Ma stepped out on the front porch and scolded him for raising a ruckus. Ma Charles, who had been sitting on the porch in the pine rocker her father made, called out to the bloodhound and joined the noisy welcome, shaking the tambourine that she always kept nearby. Knowing my great-grandmother, she probably told the dog, "Go on, boy. Wake the dead." One of the funniest things about being down home was that when Big Ma said, "Stop," Ma Charles said, "Keep on." All the pieces of down home came flooding up to greet me.

Uncle D stopped the truck and he and I got out. He went around to lift Vonetta and Fern out of the truck bed. My sisters and I became six knees in shorts galloping toward our grandmother. Before she had time to scold and fuss,

Vonetta, Fern, and I were on her, circling her, squeezing her and feeling her squeeze us. Yes, we were surely missed. I took it all in: the firm but biscuit-doughy feel of Big Ma's arms; her gardenia talcum powder and Dixie Peach hair grease dabbed under her wig around her temples. It was good to be circled by hands that smelled of pine cleaner and to be blotted by her coffee-breath kisses.

When Big Ma couldn't stand another squeeze, she pushed us off of her and said, "Let's not carry on for all the neighbors," although the only neighbor within any visible range was Mr. Lucas.

"Come on, rascals!" our great-grandmother cried, her arms stretched outward. We ran over and hugged her, but carefully. Big Ma's mother was wiry and upright but tender-skinned and small-boned. She rapped us all on the tops of our heads, one, two, three, and said, "Look at my young'ns," as if there were an army of us. "Just look at you! All those heads inching to the sky."

"All right, all right. Let's look at them inside." Big Ma was anxious to not be seen. It was too late. Mr. Lucas's house sat less than a half acre beyond the vegetable garden to our right side. He leaned against one of the white posts that ran from his porch to his roof, and he waved to us and called out to Big Ma. Big Ma waved her arms but only to tell her neighbor, "Stop that waving."

She said to Uncle Darnell, "Go drive that rig back over to him before he comes down here."

"Can't," he said. "I need to get to town." Uncle D and

Mr. Lucas had worked out an arrangement to share the truck even though Mr. Lucas hardly drove it.

Big Ma scolded us. "See what you all started up?"

Mr. Lucas didn't have as much land as my great-grandmother, but he had a few fruit trees and pecan trees on his property. The last time we drove down south, he had planted a pecan tree in Ma Charles's yard for shade. That pecan tree was hardly the same tree he'd planted a few years ago. The tree was full of pecans and its trunk and branches were now good for climbing. I couldn't hide my smile. Between the tree's height, sturdiness, and branches that formed a seat, I knew I'd found my hiding place.

Ma Charles took her time to bend down to scratch Caleb's ear. "That's a good dog. Let 'em know across the creek that I have young'ns. Let them know my roots aren't cursed. Sing, boy. Go sing! That'll show her!" Caleb raised his throat and snout and did just that while Vonetta and Fern petted him.

"Ma! Will you hush about a curse!"

Ma Charles ignored her daughter. "That's right! Sing, boy. Sing so *she* knows we have life on this side of the creek. Sing!"

Uncle D dropped our bags on the porch and said, "I'm going to town for spark plugs. I'm taking Mr. Lucas with me."

"You take him into town," Big Ma said. "But make sure you tell him tonight's for family. Just family."

Ma Charles said, "Son, tell him no such unkindness."

And Uncle D, who was probably used to being between his mother and grandmother, was already in the truck.

Fern hopped from her left foot to her right, doing her "Gotta, gotta" dance, and Vonetta hopped along with her. They both looked around for a dreaded but familiar sight. I did too.

I asked what we all needed to know. "Ma Charles, where's the moon house?" That's what we called the small blue wooden shack with half-moons painted on its front door and sides.

"The outhouse?" Ma Charles threw her head back and laughed. "The outhouse is gone," she said.

"Then where do we go?" Vonetta asked.

Ma Charles said, "Go where you want."

"Don't tell them that, Ma!" Big Ma scolded. "In spite of that no-mothering mother of theirs, they're not savages." Big Ma swatted Vonetta on the bottom, then Fern, which was as playful as Big Ma got. "Go on in the house. Use the bathroom."

Vonetta and Fern screamed for joy. They didn't want to see that outhouse any more than I wanted to iron cotton sheets.

"Nothing scarier than going to the outhouse in the spooky nighttime with the crickets chirping," Vonetta said.

"And a hoot owl going, '*Whoo-whooo*' while you're trying to make doo-doo."

"Last one waits!" Vonetta shouted. Then they raced each other into the house, leaving the bags for me to carry inside.

Last time we were here Fern was five and too scared to go to the outhouse. She used a pot instead, and my job was to dump it all down the hole inside the little moon house. And for a long while Vonetta called Fern "Stinkpot."

When we went inside the house I asked Ma Charles, "What happened to it?"

"Mr. Lucas came over one day a year ago, took down the outhouse, and put in all the pipes and pumps and such. Next thing you know, we have indoor plumbing through and through. Always had running water, but this was a welcome change."

"That was nice of him," I said. It was more than nice. I was relieved to not have to go to the moon house, or walk Vonetta there and stand guard, or carry Fern's pot there for dumping. Besides, I was a Brooklyn girl. But as sure as I couldn't stop calling my father Pa, I knew I had a small bit of the South in me too. It was funny. You don't know something bothers you until you no longer have to do it. Suddenly you're both angry and glad. Angry you did it for all those years and glad you'll never do it again.

When you get older and taller, everything else gets smaller. But not Ma Charles's house. The house was actually bigger, inside and out. It wasn't my imagination.

33

"What happened to the house? How did it get bigger?"

"What a dumb question," Vonetta said. "Houses don't grow."

"Not like daisies."

My rolling eyeballs spoke for me.

Ma Charles said, "House grew some." She turned to Big Ma and said, "No thanks to anyone under this roof."

Eyeball-rolling was catching. My grandmother rolled her eyes at her mother—something I'd never do to Cecile, and out of respect, not to Mrs., either.

"What do I know about adding on rooms, Ma?" our grandmother said innocently. "I'm a woman, not a lumberjack." Vonetta and Fern thought that was especially funny and cackled. Big Ma said, "If Elijah Lucas wants to put in plumbing and add a room or two onto your house, that's his business."

Ma Charles was disgusted by her answer. "That's not the point—whether you swing a hammer or not, daughter. The point is one day you'll step out on that back porch and smell Elijah's new wife's pecan pie cooling from her windowsill."

"She can bake shoofly pies for all I care," Big Ma said. "If Elijah wants to kill the memory of his wife and marry some woman, that's between him, God, and that some woman."

Ma Charles waved her hand away like she had no use for Big Ma.

34

I had once overheard Big Ma telling Pa he need not worry about her remarrying. She didn't want two husbands in heaven. Only one. That's why she didn't remarry after Grandpa Louis died, and that was when Pa was twelve and Uncle Darnell had been just born. Grandpa Louis died four years after he'd come home from liberating Italy along with the all-black army, according to Big Ma. He gave his medal to Pa, and Pa had given it to Uncle D when he went to Vietnam. Although no one spoke of it, Uncle D had put the medal in the pawnshop when he was sick and moaning, rattling around like a ghost. The medal was more than twenty years old and Grandpa Louis had been gone for about twenty years.

Big Ma didn't seem to mind being alone for so long. She had us and a picture of Grandpa Louis. And when she wasn't with us in Brooklyn she had Ma Charles, Uncle Darnell, and the Lord. She didn't need another husband. "No sir," she said. "One husband's all the Lord and I know about."

JimmyTROTTER,
No Space iN Between

Who needed a rooster in the morning when the Alabama sun rose early and bright to ruin my plans of sleeping until noon? It wasn't yet six o'clock but my eyes were fully open, my mind too far from dreaminess to be pulled back into sleep. Not that Big Ma would let me sleep late. Pa had told Big Ma over the phone to let us run around and have fun and to not work us half to death, even though I knew Big Ma had a special chore waiting for me. Sooner or later, I'd have to face it.

I tried to lie around but neither my mind nor body would cooperate. I sat up.

Vonetta and Fern slept at opposite ends of their twin bed, their mouths wide open as they snored into each other's feet. They were still worn out from a day and a half of bumping along on the Greyhound. I couldn't imagine that either of my sisters' legs, backs, and rumps ached more than mine. They couldn't have needed to stretch more than I did through those nine hundred miles—although Vonetta's legs were growing longer. But not as long as mine.

I tiptoed out of our room, and then past Big Ma and Ma Charles, who shared a bedroom, even though Mr. Lucas had added on a large bedroom in the back for Big Ma as well as the bathroom.

There weren't any coffee smells to fill the morning air, which meant no one was awake to ask me to do things. Although Pa didn't intend for me to work hard, Big Ma had been promising to hand down the task of ironing Ma Charles's bedsheets to me since the last time we came south. Ma Charles had her own peculiarities and didn't sleep on wrinkled sheets. My great-grandmother's bedsheets had to be white, cotton, and lightly pressed with lavender-scented Argo starch. No matter how hot it got, Big Ma had to iron white cotton sheets with light starch. "Just you wait," Big Ma said when I was nine, mopping her wet brow. "This will be your special job when you all come down here next." I grew to hate the sight of white sheets.

I unlocked and opened the screen door gently to step out onto the back porch without it creaking.

Not only had Ma Charles's house grown, but the hen-house and the chicken run had also expanded. For one thing, we had more chickens. A little more than a dozen. The henhouse wasn't the small, red painted box I remembered, but was now large enough to enter standing fully upright. The new chicken run was made to give the chickens room to spread out. The house, the dog, the pecan tree, the henhouse, and the chicken run had all sprung up or spread outward. They didn't *seem* bigger. They *were* bigger.

I went to unlatch the lock to the henhouse but it was already undone, the door cracked ajar. The smell of straw, chicken feathers, and chicken droppings rose up to my nose. I peered through the opening without entering, although I knew that wiry scarecrow form, stooped over the row of hens squatting in small dresser drawer–like boxes. The hens didn't even stir when he took their eggs. He had an easy way about him. His back was to me but he didn't bother to turn around. He didn't have to. I knew he heard me or felt my shadow in the door crack, just like I knew he was smiling. He placed an egg in his basket and straightened up.

"Hey, Cousin Del."

I opened the door wide and he came to greet me. I was so happy to see him, I couldn't stop grinning. JimmyTrotter was three years older than me but we'd always been the same height. Now, he'd shot past me and was as tall as Pa and Uncle Darnell.

"It could have been Big Ma, Ma Charles, or Uncle D. How'd you know it was me?"

"You're a country girl at heart. Up with the sun."

"Not me," I said. "I'd sleep all day long if I could."

He placed the basket of eggs down on the straw-covered ground and gave me a good and proper hug, and then he dug his knuckle on top of my head to show me he was taller, in case I hadn't noticed. Then I knuckled him in the rib to show him I was from Brooklyn and didn't take any mess from a country boy, older cousin or not.

Cousin JimmyTrotter. At school and on paper his name was a properly spaced James Trotter. At home among family was another story altogether. For reasons that had more to do with his great-grandmother and mine, he answered to "JimmyTrotter." No space in between.

I couldn't imagine dragging my last name with me from sunup to sundown, but JimmyTrotter and his great-grandmother wouldn't have it any other way. I'd tried to give my cousin a shorter, tougher, Brooklyn-styled nickname, JT. He'd said firmly without his good-natured ease, "You can call me cuz or cousin. Whichever. But call me JimmyTrotter or don't call me." And he meant it.

We pulled apart from each other, laughing.

"Your grandmother said you and your sisters were coming down. It was all she talked about for weeks."

Good to know we were wanted! But to my cousin I said, "Well, we made it," like the journey was nothing.

"You sure did." He looked me up and down and said, "How'd you get so pretty so fast, cuz? Thought it would take at least another five or six years."

I hated myself for blushing. That compliment made him seem much older, like he was giving a penny candy to an anxious little kid. I played it off by changing the subject. "Look at all these chickens! At least fourteen hens." I went inside the small, dark room.

"Sixteen," he said. "The reds are Aunt Naomi's. The light browns . . . well, they *were* Mr. Lucas's." It was always weird to hear him call Ma Charles "Aunt Naomi" and Big Ma "Aunt Ophelia" and even weirder to remember they had names of their own, although I never used them.

"He sold them to Ma Charles?"

"Sold. Gave. The girls all get along and the eggs keep coming. And if chicken is on the menu, Mr. Lucas makes a run to the chicken and feed store for replacements. All girls, of course." He thumped me on the shoulder. "Pick up a basket and help me, unless you don't know how."

"I know my way around a coop," I said, although I didn't really want to stick my hands beneath any feathered chicken butts.

JimmyTrotter wouldn't let me forget the eggs I dropped and cracked when I was nine. "If you crack 'em, they're your breakfast eggs."

"Not hardly."

Maybe my hands were cold but the hen began to flap when I reached for her egg.

"Easy, easy, cuz." He shook his head, like, *Sure, you know your way around a coop.* JimmyTrotter reminded me of Pa, and he resembled the photograph of Grandpa Louis Gaither that Big Ma kept on her dresser too much to not be a Gaither. And he was both Hershey's brown and clay red and too good-looking to be my cousin. I felt myself blushing.

"Now that we're here I'll bet you're glad you don't have to be up to bring the milk *and* collect the eggs."

"You'd be wrong about that, cuz."

I gave him *Say what?* eyebrows and he smiled, knowing what I didn't know.

"Stick around, cuz. It's actually fun."

"Fun?"

"Or funny," he said. "Not the cows or the chickens. Miss Trotter and Aunt Naomi."

Our great-grandmothers, Ruth and Naomi Trotter.

"Oh, really?"

"Keep your ears open, cuz. You'll catch on."

"Why not just tell me what's going on?"

"Gotta have my fun," JimmyTrotter said. "There's an art to doing it."

"Doing what?"

"Giving them just enough of what they want but not too much."

"Enough what?" I asked.

"I'll give you a day or two. You'll catch on."

StRaight fRom Sophie

Even though my cousin was bent on flaunting his age and height over me, I relished the time I spent with him apart from my sisters. What a difference three years made between us. We could barely stand each other at nine and twelve. Now he was practically a grown man. Sitting on the back porch yapping with my fifteen-year-old cousin made me feel like the teenager I'd soon be in October.

We could both smell coffee brewing in the kitchen. The house was waking up. He gave my shoulder a light tap instead of a thump and said, "Let's go inside."

Soon there would be noise and chores and a mountain of white sheets with my name on them to wash, hang dry, and iron. I wasn't looking forward to it but I went in with him.

Vonetta and Fern came alive at the table the minute they saw Cousin JimmyTrotter.

"Straight from Sophie," he said, placing a heavy quart bottle of milk on the kitchen table. I carried the basket full of small brown and white eggs.

"Who's Sophie?" Fern asked, but no one answered.

"Cold milk!" Vonetta cried. "In time for cornflakes!"

"Cornflakes?" Ma Charles said. "Cornflakes won't put meat on those bony bones." She turned to Big Ma and said, "Daughter, stir those grits up right. Extra hunk of butter—good butter from McDaniels's farm," she felt the need to add. "And bring out the ham and biscuits. These gals have been starving. See how they've wasted away."

Vonetta said, "I want cornflakes. Great-grandma Charles, I know you have them."

"And I don't want ham," Fern whined.

Big Ma said, "That's not how I raised you two—telling your elders what you want and don't want. Just as unmannerly as a seal on strike at the circus."

"May I please have lots of milk with my cornflakes?" It was too fake and sweet for Vonetta.

"If that's how you want to waste away, it's all right with me," Ma Charles said.

"Yes, ma'am, thank you, ma'am." Fern called up all

the southern talk she knew. "I'll waste away on milk and cornflakes too. But please, ma'am, more cornflakes than milk and no thank you, ma'am, to pig ham."

Big Ma said we would cause her slow and unmerciful death, but we knew she didn't mean it.

Vonetta took the thick bottle of milk with both hands. "Why is it so warm?" she asked. "Milk's supposed to be cold."

"Like I said, cuz. It's straight from Sophie," JimmyTrotter said.

"Who's Sophie?" Fern asked again, but no one answered.

Vonetta pruned up her face. "Straight from Sophie. That sounds nasty."

"Where do you think milk comes from?" I asked her.

"The store. In a red and white carton."

"With a picture of a cow on a farm," Fern said.

"That farm's across the creek," JimmyTrotter said. "That cow is Sophie. And in a month, that milk'll come from Butter."

"That makes no sense," Vonetta said. "Everyone knows butter comes from milk, not the other way around."

"You tell him!" Ma Charles said.

Vonetta went on. "As long as I can have my cornflakes, I'll take the milk straight from the cow. Just get here sooner and stick the bottle in the freezer."

I was ready to kick Vonetta under the table but Big Ma told her to watch herself. JimmyTrotter laughed his head off and told her she was funny and cute.

"As long as—" Fern started to follow Vonetta, but stopped herself. "Cousin JimmyTrotter. Is it all right with Sophie? Us drinking her milk?"

"It sure is, cuz." He answered so easily she had no choice but to believe him.

Ma Charles shook her head, amused and surprised by Fern's question. "If that don't beat all."

Then Fern finished her thought. "As long as the cow says, 'Mooo,' I'll drink it tooo."

"All this talk about where milk comes from," Ma Charles said. "Milk comes from a cow. Maybe a goat. In all my eighty-two years I never drank a drop of factory milk and I won't start now. Never had an egg come out of a carton or a loaf of bread that didn't rise up in my oven, and furthermore, it's a sin to throw a nickel on a head of cabbage or a bunch of carrots that already grows up out of my own dirt."

"Thank you, Claretha Darrow," Big Ma said. Claretha must have been Aretha Franklin's pulpit-preaching twin, for all we knew: Big Ma, like Ma Charles, was on a roll. She was funniest when she didn't mean to make us laugh. "You all haven't been down home a full minute and you're already raising Mama's pressure and mine along with hers."

Ma Charles tsk-tsked about how lean and undernourished JimmyTrotter looked and then told him to sit down.

"Your old great-granny is in such poor health she can't rise up from her death bed to feed you."

JimmyTrotter winked at me and said to Ma Charles, "Miss Trotter's far from her deathbed, Auntie. She gets around and cooks plenty. I know because I eat plenty."

"I doubt she gets around, as old and sickly as she is," Ma Charles insisted.

"Mama!" Big Ma scolded. "You two are the same age."

"Twins!" Vonetta exclaimed. "You're twin sisters. I hope twins run in the family. I'm having twins."

"You're having breakfast," is what Big Ma said. "Never mind no twins."

"Twins nothing," Ma Charles said, truly riled by the thought. "My mama had me first. Her mama had her second. You tell her that," she ordered. JimmyTrotter gave her a "Yes'm, Auntie," and threw me another sly wink.

"Do you hear this?" Big Ma said. "Stop telling the family business."

"Aren't we the family?" Fern asked.

JimmyTrotter said, "Don't worry about Miss Trotter. Great-granny goes out with her deer rifle. Can still pick off a rabbit every now and then."

"What's that to me?" Ma Charles said, but she was now ruffled at being contradicted. "I fish the wide end of the creek and tend that garden."

"Ma, you haven't gone—"

But Ma Charles waved her hand to tell Big Ma to hush

and continued to speak over her. "You tell her I said there's no shame in using that cane I sent her. Pride goeth before the fall." I caught my great-grandmother half rolling her eyes.

"Miss Trotter's just fine, Auntie," he said, although she was his great-aunt. "And she wants to know if your rheumatism's any better. If you need another bottle of ginger and goldenseal."

"Ma don't need any Indian roots and berries," Big Ma said. "She needs to see about her sister."

"I know about my half sister, all right," Ma Charles snapped real fast. "I know all about her."

Fern whispered in a weak voice, "She hunts deer? And rabbits?"

Vonetta held up her fork as if it had a trigger and a barrel. I slapped the fork down and dared Vonetta to do something about it.

Then Uncle Darnell came into the kitchen and said, "Ma, you packed my lunchbox? My thermos?" Big Ma was especially happy to fuss over her son. When Uncle Darnell looked toward Vonetta, she turned her face away and chomped on her cereal as hard as she could.

Far from Net-Net and Unc

You would think that having all of us together would heal old wounds. After three nights of gathering around Ma Charles's table for supper, Vonetta wouldn't soften. Uncle Darnell stopped looking her way while he told stories about his job at the textile mill over in Prattville. He stopped waiting for her to chuckle at the funny parts or give him the smallest forgiving sign. He finally said as he passed the biscuit platter, "Vonetta, I've already apologized. I was a different man then. But as far as I'm concerned I've made amends. That's all you get." And when he passed the gravy boat her way, he could have been passing it to anyone but his favorite niece.

* * *

"Vonetta." Fern and I ganged up on her before nighttime reading, prayer, and lights-out. Vonetta rolled cow eyes up at us in place of answering as we stood over her.

"You make me sick," I told her.

"You make me sicker," she snapped back.

The quickness of her reply made Fern go, "Oooh."

"Uncle was sick. He's better now. Or he's getting better."

"And he's sorry," Fern said.

Vonetta fired off another one. "He broke my jar and stole my money." From the shine in her eyes, it might as well have still been the Sunday afternoon that we had come home from church and found the jar broken and all the concert money gone, except for a few coins. "I didn't get to see Michael, Marlon, Jermaine, Tito, or Jackie at Madison Square Garden." She pointed a finger on one hand for each Jackson and was breathing hard when she'd stopped naming and pointing.

The disappointment and loss of not going to the concert suddenly overwhelmed Fern. "Yeah. We didn't see Michael."

"It wasn't just your money," I told Vonetta's stubborn lip. "It was ours. All of ours. And *we* didn't get to see the Jackson Five. We."

"We surely didn't." Fern slid back to my side. I knew I could count on her for support.

"You weren't the only one who missed the Jackson Five," I told her.

"Surely weren't."

"Uncle said he was sorry, Vonetta. And he means it. He's better."

Vonetta's neck went rolling along with her cow eyes. "If you want to accept his sorry, then go ahead, you sorry, sorry sisters." And then she stood up to me like she was going to slug me. Vonetta had grown taller but not tall enough to stand eye to eye with me. She still had to look up.

"You'll be sorry in a minute," I warned her.

She stepped even closer. "Oh yeah?"

She pushed me with all her might and I tottered back a step but not much. I gave her a hard, swift push and she fell onto the bed. Then she let out her war cry, just like she did when she hollered in her crib. That only told me she was fueling up to spring back, so I met her fast and shoved her back down onto the bed. Uncle charged into in the room and pulled me off of her.

"What are you two fighting about?"

Big Ma was right behind him. "Don't let me get my strap. Carrying on like hopping mad kangaroos in a boxing match. Delphine, you know better than to jump on your baby sister."

Fern took offense. "*I'm* the baby sister. She's the old middle."

Before Vonetta could answer to being called the old middle, Uncle said louder, "I asked you, what were you two fighting about?"

I didn't say anything and neither did Vonetta. But that didn't stop Fern.

"Vonetta said she—"

Uncle Darnell held up his hand. "Didn't ask you, Li'l Bit. I asked them."

We both said in almost one voice, "Nothing."

"Wild," Big Ma scolded. "Just wild. Send them to Oakland to see their mother and they come back wild. Your father brings Miss Women's Lib into the house spouting her nonsense and my grands they think they're wild and free. No one knows how to be a young lady. No sir. No one knows how to be a young lady."

"At least you still know how to be an old lady, Big Ma." I do believe Fern meant to say something nice.

Uncle laughed and Big Ma swatted Fern's backside, but not really. Not like a whipping. I felt myself easing up but Vonetta stayed tight-lipped with arms crossed.

"Shake," Uncle told us. "Go on."

"You can't tell me what to do," Vonetta sniped.

Then Big Ma, who'd been jollied out of her fussing, was once again sharp and angry. "You're asking for my strap but my backhand will do just fine," she told Vonetta.

Uncle said to Vonetta, "I'm your uncle, not your equal. Don't you ever mouth off to me. Do you hear me, girl?" All I could think was how far from "Net-Net and Unc" they'd become. Now Uncle Darnell was more like Papa than Papa.

51

Vonetta nodded, but Uncle Darnell wouldn't take her nod like he might have done before. Back when he was young with a face full of dimples and danced the Watusi even when that dance had been long out of style. He said, "What was that?"

"Yes." The word dragged and hissed out of her mouth.

"Yes, what?" he asked.

"Yes, sir."

I knew Vonetta was hurt to have to "sir" Uncle Darnell when Papa had only made us "sir" him once that I could remember. Neither Vonetta, Fern, nor I liked saying "Yes, sir." "Yes, sir" was how Big Ma told us we'd better answer a white man, no matter how young or old he was.

"Now, shake," Uncle Darnell said again.

Vonetta stuck her hand out to me and I shook it. Then we pulled our hands apart.

Chicken Run

I loved my view, holed up in the woodsy Y of our pecan tree's branches surrounded by nothing but pointed green leaves and pecan clusters still shelled in green husks. It was so peaceful I didn't even bother to swat flies or gnats. The pecan tree made the perfect reading spot, with its far-reaching arms and its cradle high enough to keep me above fighting sisters or Big Ma when wash day came around. As long as my sisters couldn't climb its trunk to get to the cradle, I'd always have a place to go.

I decided I was done with *Things Fall Apart* for now. No one had to know I'd grown tired of reading it. Instead, I followed *The Soul Brothers and Sister Lou* on their way to becoming a singing group in Philadelphia. That was more my speed. And Sister Lou? I might as well be inside her skin.

After sailing through a few chapters of my book, I took a break to slow the story a bit. I didn't mean to spy on Fern but I couldn't help watch her down below in the chicken run with her new friends. Ma Charles gave her the job of gathering up chicken poop for the garden, and Fern went right to work with a garden spade and a dust pan.

Between the pecking hens and the chicken-poop smell, I couldn't get Fern to go near the henhouse when she was five—let alone inside the chicken run. Now she spoke to the chickens, expecting them to understand her. So when Big Ma had announced she'd be baking chicken for tonight's supper, I saw the gears turning in Fern's mind. She was up to something.

She left the run to grab a twig that had fallen from the pecan tree. I watched her poke her hand with its tip to test its sharpness. She marched back inside the run like she had been a chicken feeder and egg collector all her life. The hens paid her no mind, seeing that she came with a crooked stick and no feed. They let her do what was on her mind to do.

Fern pushed the straw aside in the center of the run to reveal patches of grass but mostly dirt. She bent down with her twig in hand and began to write in the dirt, all the while shooing her hens away. I couldn't tell what she wrote but whatever it was, she took a second to admire it and clunked her turtle head, congratulating herself. Now, I had to know. I inched out farther and leaned over. From what I could see, Fern had scratched out chicken feet. Big chicken feet. I wanted to tell her that chicken feet aren't that big, but she seemed proud of her work so I said nothing.

She talked to her hens. "Now, Henny Pennics," she said, "I'm doing this for your own good. When Big Ma comes out here, just look smart."

The hens clucked back.

Then she called out, "Big Ma! Big Ma! Come quick!"

Big Ma didn't post herself up in the door frame immediately, so Fern left the run, but not without warning her chickens, "Look smart, Henny Pennies. Extra smart!" She framed hand goggles around her eyes and pressed her face against the back door screen. "Big Ma! Come here! Come here! I have something stupendous to show you. Unbelievably stupendous."

Finally Big Ma appeared, her hands caked with flour, her face puzzled. "What?"

Fern pointed to the chicken run with one hand and motioned, *Come on, come on,* with the other. She jumped away from the door. "You have to come out and see, Big Ma!"

Big Ma cracked the screen door but remained inside. She had no time to fool with Fern, but Fern stamped her foot, confounded by the effort it took to get Big Ma near the chicken run. She pointed to her chicken-feet drawing, and waited for Big Ma to be unbelievably astounded.

"Fern Gaither, what are you trying to show me?"

There was a commotion in the chicken run, but not the spectacle that Fern had in mind. Some insect, maybe a grasshopper or worm, found its way to the center of the chicken run and all the chickens went crazy pecking, flapping, and scratching to get at it. Fern's chicken-feet etching had all but eroded in the pecking frenzy. Still, Fern pointed to what was left of the twig scratchings like the drawing was as clear as day.

"Free Hens!" she cried.

Big Ma's face scrunched in on itself. *"What?"*

"Free Hens! Like 'Free Huey!'"

"Don't start up that Black Panther mess down here. Not today. Not any day."

"No, Big Ma," Fern said. "You're not seeing it."

"Seeing what, child?"

By now, Fern's arms were crossed, and that was not the right way to get Big Ma to see anything, especially when Big Ma had other things to do. "Like in *Charlotte's Web*. These are *some* chickens," she said, expecting Big Ma to have read *Charlotte's Web* and to get her meaning.

"I know they're some chickens," Big Ma said. "There's going be one less chicken after supper."

"No, Big Ma. You can't. You can't."

I expected Big Ma to shoo Fern off to play. But Big

Ma marched around to the door of the wire chicken run and snatched up a plump, light brown hen. If I had been inside, instead of up in my tree, Big Ma would have sent me out to the run to get a good-size pullet and bring it to her—lifeless, still warm, and ready for plucking. This was how I knew not to name a chicken, even the ones that strutted around the run as if they had a name. But Big Ma pushed past Fern, grabbed "Bertha," snapped her neck while her light-brown-feathered body fussed about before stopping cold, and brought supper into the house. The screen door slammed.

Fern stood there. Arms crossed. Then arms down at her side. Fists balled. She wound herself up and marched to the screen door, put her face against the screen, and yelled, "Chicken killer! Chicken killer!"

I didn't bother with climbing. I jumped out of the tree. *The Soul Brothers and Sister Lou* lay somewhere in the dirt. I ran and dragged my baby sister from the door.

As sure as I knew she would be, Big Ma was in the door frame in nothing flat. "Delphine. Go get me a switch."

The nearest switch was the twig Fern used to scratch the message that was supposed to save her hens.

I never disobeyed Big Ma but I wasn't about to bring her any switch. Fern was beat down enough after seeing that hen's neck snapped clean while its body did a dying funky-chicken dance. Wasn't that punishment enough? Even when I was nine and Big Ma had told me to bring her a chicken for supper I knew better than to do it in front of my sisters. I waited until Vonetta and Fern were inside taking a nap before I did my chicken killing.

At supper Fern ate bread and corn but she wouldn't touch the gravy-coated drumstick Big Ma put on her plate.

"If you don't eat that chicken you don't get any 'nana pudding."

Fern lifted her little turtle head higher instead of saying "So?" to her grandmother.

Ma Charles laughed at this war between the two. She lifted her arms. "Come on, give your great-grand a hug, you rascal."

Fern leaped out of her chair, ran around to Ma Charles, and buried her face in her neck and chest.

Big Ma wasn't pleased. "See how you do, repaying the wicked? That's not right, Ma."

"Oh, hush," Ma Charles said, burying Fern in all that love.

"Look at the baby," Vonetta said. She stabbed her fork into the thigh on her plate and took a big bite. "Mm. Mm. Mm. Tasty."

Tears rolled down Fern's face.

"If you're pleased to make a spectacle of yourself over chicken you been eating since you had teeth, go on to your room. You know better than to be crying at the table while hungry people are trying to take in the good Lord's bounty. All them starving children in Africa going to bed hungry. You get in your bed and have a taste of hungry along with them."

Vonetta found religion. "Amen. Tasty. Tasty."

Fern marched off to our room, her turtle head high, her fists clenched.

"It's that wife of his' doing," Big Ma said. "Women's liberation and can't boil a turnip. That woman's going to turn my girls into useless jaw-jerkers."

I expected to find Fern tummy-down, spread out on the bed and fast asleep after a bout of crying. Instead we found her sitting up with her arms folded and her neck still high. She had gone from twig-and-dirt writing to a blue fountain pen on lily wallpaper. Like our mother used to.

Books lie.
Lie. Lie. Lie.
Charlotte lied.
Webs lie.
Web of lies.
What is a word for a lie?
A story.

It was signed "Afua," the African name our mother had tried to give Fern when she was born, but Pa wouldn't let her. Now Fern was trying to be like our mother. If Cecile could have a poet's name—Nzila—then so could Fern.

I'd read her words but all I could see was blue ink over Big Ma's wallpaper.

"Ooh!" Vonetta cooed, her eyes bright with glee. "Ooh! You're gonna get it."

"Fern. You're asking for it," I said.

"So."

"You have to wash that off."

"That's my poem."

"That's not a poem," Vonetta said. "All the lines end in 'lie' except for the one that ends in 'story.' You call that a poem?"

Fern was most proud of that. All those "lies."

"It needs a rhyme with something like 'pecan pie,'" Vonetta said. "And you're gonna need a beating once Big Ma sees that ink on her wallpaper."

I hated to admit it but Vonetta was right. After a day like today, Big Ma would have gone out to the yard and found a switch herself. She would have stung Fern's legs extra hard to whip the Cecile out of her. Cecile was forever writing on walls when she lived with us, and Pa was forever painting over them.

I soaked a rag in pine cleaner and water and gave it to Fern. "Scrub," I told her. But I didn't say what Big Ma used to tell me: "Scrub like a gal in a one-cow town." I didn't want to start bringing cows into it.

* * *

In the morning, one single scrambled egg sat on Fern's plate. It, along with all the food on the table, had been blessed.

Ma Charles's eyes twinkled Fern's way. I think she liked Fern's stubborn little face. "Go on," Ma Charles said gently. "Eat your breakfast."

Hungry but turtle-headed Fern stared at the egg.

"Go on," Vonetta said. "Eat the baby chick-chick."

Ma Charles crooked her pointer finger at Vonetta. "Get back, wicked one."

Vonetta smiled, pleased with her mischief.

"Eggs are just eggs, baby," Ma Charles said, warm like Papa.

Fern looked up.

"We need a rooster to turn eggs to chicks. Tell her, daughter." She meant me, although I was her great-granddaughter.

I didn't know anything about roosters and eggs but it sounded true. I nodded.

Ma Charles winked. "Delphine studied her science in school. She knows."

That wasn't the science we learned in the sixth grade, but I wasn't going to contradict my great-grandmother, especially if Fern would begin to eat.

Fern pushed the tines of her fork into her scrambled egg. After playing in it she speared a sliver and ate it.

Vonetta waited until she swallowed. *"Buck-buck-buck-buck-kawk!"*

Ruination of Things

I couldn't, wouldn't waste another minute dreading wash day and ironing the white sheets. Maybe it was the short time I had spent with Cecile and the Black Panthers last summer. It was harder to do what I was asked without speaking up when I didn't want to do it at all. Maybe it was how Mrs. half-jokingly said, "The slaves have been freed, Delphine," whenever she saw me doing things the long, hard way. The way Big Ma had taught me. Maybe it was three years' worth of dread. I could feel things bubbling up inside of me. Besides, I saw no reason why anyone should have to starch and iron white or any other colored sheets when there were such things as wrinkle-free permanent-press sheets. I remembered how Big Ma's face turned to wet marble, her lips grim and pursed as she starched and pressed, one iron working hard up and down a sheet while the second iron sat in flames atop the stove, waiting.

I loved Ma Charles as much as I could love her without having been around her much, but I couldn't slave over those white sheets. There was something about those sheets that made me grown enough to take the whipping I had coming to me for the disrespect I was about to show my grandmother and great-grandmother.

The sun was at its highest point, which meant the sheets were dry. I made up my mind. I didn't have to be told to go and pull the sheets down off of the line. I took them down, folded them in tight rectangular squares, and brought them inside, where my grandmother, the ironing board, and two flaming irons waited for me.

I didn't have a "Free Huey!" chant to keep me brave and moving forward. Just *This is the last whipping. The last whipping.* I imagined a mob of Black Panthers saying it with me.

Deep inside I knew it wasn't the whipping I dreaded. Big Ma couldn't really hurt me with a switch or a belt. I had already felt the sting of a belt-whipping and carried each blow in my memory. And then, that was it. Once I knew how bad each blow could be I felt my skin toughen. I could take it and maybe not even sniffle. It was how Big Ma would look at me afterward that made me queasy and feel the regret. I had to speak up for myself.

"I got you started with the starch and both irons are hot. Only way to press cotton is with a hot iron." She was already sweating.

"Big Ma . . ." Everything sounded good and strong in my head. But my mouth struggled to open.

"Not too much lavender and don't let it burn. Go on."

"Big Ma . . ."

"What, child?"

"Ma'am."

"A mercy, Delphine. What is it?"

"I don't iron sheets at home. Not even Pa's shirts."

Big Ma stopped what she was doing. "Is that so?"

The last whipping. This is the last whipping.

I still couldn't look her in the eye.

Big Ma's right hand found her hip.

The last whipping. The last, last one.

"You might as well speak up. Your mouth is already open."

"Yes, Big Ma."

"The ruination of all things. The collapse and ruin of all things civil. I blame your mother. And your father. And that women's-libber. And what they're teaching and not teaching in school. I tell you, it's all falling apart. Mark my words. Children will stop minding grown people and worse. Much worse. You'd be different if you grew up here like your cousin, and not up there."

64

Instead of feeling the victory of standing up for myself, I felt tall, stupid, and worthless. Even worse when my grandmother shook the box of cornstarch into the spray bottle, spilling clumps of white powder on the floor. I bent to scoop some up but she stopped me.

"You had your say, now go on," she told me. "Take your sisters and git."

"We don't have nowhere—"

"One don't eat chicken or ham. One don't forgive. The other don't iron. Just git, Delphine. Take your sisters and git."

Great Miss Trotter

Big Ma said "Git," but there was no place to go. It wasn't as if we were in Brooklyn, where the candy store, the record shop, and my best friend were around the corner. We were in deeply wooded nowheresville, and Uncle Darnell, our only hope of getting a ride, was long gone to work and then to school. We didn't have a bike to pedal the nearly three miles to the nearest store, and even if we did, only Vonetta and I could ride a bicycle well enough. The pecan tree could hold one, maybe two of us, but only I'd be unafraid to climb it. To boot, our nearest neighbor was an older man without any kids or kids' games. I didn't know how we would stay out of Big Ma's sight. But when Ma Charles said, "That boy must have girls on his mind.

He left his great-granny's denture rinse," I said, "We'll take it over!"

"See if I care if she gets it or not," Ma Charles said, which was as good as permission to cross the creek and hike over to Miss Trotter's.

We were glad to leave Ma Charles's house, and Big Ma was especially glad to see us go. I took the canning jar filled with water, mint leaves, baking soda, and whatever else swam in it, and my sisters and I set out in the direction of the creek that separated Ma Charles from Miss Trotter.

I knew the way to Miss Trotter's but my sisters had never been. I'd crossed the wooden walkway over the creek with Pa when we last came down for the Trotter funerals. Vonetta and Fern weren't up to walking that far so it was only Pa and me, and I wanted to show him I could keep up with him.

Now that they were older and bored, Vonetta and Fern were glad to take the short hike. We walked across the dried grass field dotted with purple flowers until there were none. Just bugs that kept us slapping our legs and arms. Then we continued on through the skinny pines, more open fields, a little less than half a mile before we crossed the old wooden planks. Pa said his great-grandfather, Slim Jim Trotter, built that old crossing, which turned out to be part of his undoing. I had asked him what he meant by that and he said, "Nothing you need to know right now."

Once over the walkway we took a path too small for a car, but perfect for a horse, a bicycle, or for walking.

I recognized Miss Trotter instantly when we approached the house made of wood. She sat spine-straight like Ma Charles on the porch, in her chair—the same handmade wooden chair as Ma Charles had. Her eyes seemed to be closed so we approached carefully, to not startle her. When she did open her eyes we wanted to give her a hug or say, "Hi, Auntie!" but she didn't smile or hold out her arms. If she didn't mirror Ma Charles so much, we would have kept walking.

She inhaled deeply, lifted her pointer finger to the air, and said, "Feel that? The warm and the cool?"

"It's hot to me, Miss Trotter," I said, smiling. I was sweating to prove it.

"Burning hot," Fern added.

Somehow we disappointed our great-aunt, Miss Trotter. She was already shaking her head no. "You're talking about the sun. I'm talking about the air."

"Doesn't the sun heat the air?" I asked.

"The sun isn't the wind," she said.

Fern and I shrugged, but good old mouthy Vonetta spoke up. "What's the difference?"

"The difference? If you have to ask I might as well not tell you the difference."

What do you say to that? I held out the jar with green mint leaves. "For your dentures, from Ma Charles."

"Dentures? Dentures?" She bared her teeth to show them but not to smile. "Go on. Run your finger 'longside the uppers and lowers. You can go all the way back if you want to."

"No, thank you, Miss Trotter," I said. I didn't mean to be rude but "No, thank you" was better than what I kept from coming out of my mouth. After all, she was an elder and the second-oldest Trotter—according to Ma Charles.

"You tell her . . ." *Her* was Ma Charles—our great-grandmother, Miss Trotter's half sister. "Tell her my teeth are just fine. Why would a wolf need more teeth than the ones she already has?" She peered suspiciously at the greenish mixture, and I couldn't blame her for making a face. "Denture rinse. I got something for her. You wait."

She talked on and on while we stared. Miss Trotter and our great-grandmother were crowned by the same gray-and-black hair, but it was styled differently to suit them. Miss Trotter's hair was loosely parted and braided in pigtails. Ma Charles's hair was finely parted down the middle and pooled in a bun and hairnet. Their cheek-bones made their faces seem long, although Ma Charles's face was slightly rounder, a feature both she and Big Ma inherited from Great-great-grandmother Livonia Trotter. I knew this from the brownish faded photograph of Livonia and Slim Jim Trotter that sat on the china cabinet next to an all-watchful Jesus. When I had come over with Pa to deliver our condolences personally I had seen what I thought was the same picture as the one that sat on the china cabinet in Ma Charles's house. I'd been fooled because my great-great-grandfather wore the same suit and the same grim face in both photographs, his hair thick and long. The only difference in both pictures was the bride standing next to him. I didn't think too much of it back then, but now I could see how the wooden crossing over the creek might have led to my great-great-grandfather's undoing.

Except for the funerals I can't say I remember my great-aunt and great-grandmother being under the same roof or together under the same piece of sky. Their resemblance was closer than that of my sisters and me, and we looked alike. It didn't seem right that Miss Trotter and Ma Charles didn't visit or speak directly to each other when they were half sisters.

Pa had told me their relationship had always been strained. He'd said that when it was time to take care of the funeral arrangements and the repast three years ago, Ma Charles had to step in and handle everything because Miss Trotter wasn't able. After that, instead of things getting better between the half sisters, they only grew worse.

JimmyTrotter must have heard us, and he came out of his room and onto the porch to greet us. His hands smelled like strong glue. Fern coughed, and he brushed his hands against his pants and said by way of apology and explanation, "Model-airplane glue."

Miss Trotter couldn't understand how we couldn't feel the cool moisture in the air. She passed her thumb over her fingertips. "Feel it, JimmyTrotter?"

"Yes'm. Sure do." But he said it so quick and plain I was sure he didn't feel a thing.

Miss Trotter was satisfied with his answer. "Good." She clunked her head the way Fern does when she's proud of herself or when she knows she's right. "Good. At least you won't get caught in the storm."

"The weatherman didn't say storm," I said.

She said, "The president didn't say higher taxes, but anyone with eyes can see what's coming around the corner."

Vonetta seemed too awestruck by Miss Trotter to cheer my being put in my place by our elder. She gazed at Miss Trotter and kept her smart Vonetta sass to herself. I knew that look on her face. She gave the same hungry and hopeful gaze to new kids moving into the neighborhood, hoping to find a friend among them.

Fern wasn't impressed by our great-aunt. She said, "We want to see the cows, Aunt Miss Trotter. Now."

"Miss Trotter," our great-aunt stated.

"You're our aunt," Fern said.

"Great-aunt," I whispered.

"Miss Trotter," our great-aunt insisted. "That'll do. But

I might answer to Great Miss Trotter if you want to be respectful."

Vonetta finally showed signs of life. "Yes, Great Miss Trotter."

Fern wasn't satisfied. "We want an aunt," she said, one fist balled. "JimmyTrotter has an Auntie Naomi and an Aunt Ophelia. Two aunties. We want one Aunt Miss Trotter."

"I thought you wanted to see a cow," Miss Trotter said.

"Surely do."

"Then go on." Miss Trotter pointed her chin to the field past the barn. "Go see your cow."

"Come on," JimmyTrotter said, smiling. He was amused that Fern annoyed and confounded his great-grandmother. "Butter and Sophie are over there." He pointed to where the cows were resting. Fern took off running toward the black-and-white cows and so did Vonetta, but not before she curtsied and said, "See you later, Great Miss Trotter!"

Sophie's On

I followed JimmyTrotter inside, where he washed the glue smell off his hands. Then we went out to the patch of grass where Sophie and Butter lay, and he got Sophie up and led her to the barn. I didn't know if it was a good idea to have Vonetta and Fern see where milk came from since they drank it every day, but they were excited to watch JimmyTrotter milk Sophie.

He walked her to a post with a rope and tied the rope loosely around her neck. "My dad rigged this harness when Auggie and me . . ." He didn't finish. He didn't have to. I could see that JimmyTrotter didn't talk about his brother, mother, father, or grandmother or the accident caused by the oncoming trucker who had fallen asleep at the wheel while driving a tractor-trailer carrying lumber. Every Trotter in the car had been killed, all at once. A stomach virus had kept JimmyTrotter at home with Miss Trotter that day. Now he was the only one left to carry the Trotter name—and he carried it with him, all right. Well, he and Miss Trotter.

I didn't know what to say.

I pointed to the leather hanging from the post. "And that makes it easier?"

He loosened the strap. "Safer," he said. "I don't normally use it. Sophie stands easy for me. But she's not used to an audience."

"That's hurting her," Fern said.

"I wouldn't do it if it was," JimmyTrotter said. He placed his stool at Sophie's right side, put two metal pails beneath her, and sat down. The first pail was half-filled with warm water and a little soap. He took a rag, dipped it into the soap water, and washed Sophie's udder. The girls started to giggle.

"You don't want dirty milk, do you?"

They only giggled more.

When he was sure Sophie was clean enough, he rubbed his hands together and then grabbed two of the hanging parts and left the other two dangling. We made faces as he pulled down and squeezed. Pulled and squeezed.

"Poor Sophie," Fern said.

"She'd kick me right now if we weren't friends," JimmyTrotter said.

"Ewwww," Vonetta said when the thin white stream shot out into the pail. I could have said it along with her but didn't.

"This won't take too long. I only have to milk Sophie for now."

"Why?" Fern asked. She told him it was unfair that one cow got milked and the other just sat out in the sun chewing grass.

"Sophie's on and Butter's off—but not for long!"

Fern laughed and repeated after him, "Sophie's on and Butter's off."

"Sophie's a champion milking cow, although I think she's getting ready to taper off. Don't worry." He smiled a warm JimmyTrotter smile. "Today's a good day. Sophie girl's set to show off for you. About three gallons' worth." He lowered his voice and added, "She only calved a few months back," as if he said something the cow shouldn't hear. "I'm hoping she'll be good for another couple of months, but I don't know."

"Calved?" Fern asked.

"It means she had a cow," Vonetta snapped.

JimmyTrotter turned his head away from Sophie to shoot Vonetta a look. "Don't say it like that. Fern doesn't know and neither do you."

"Surely don't," Fern said.

Vonetta turned up her nose.

"So where's the baby cow?" Fern asked.

"Calf," Vonetta corrected. "Calf."

"He's on a special farm," JimmyTrotter said fast and plain, like when he "Yes'm-ed" Miss Trotter about the cool in the air. "A special farm for tender, young cows."

Fern thought that was swell. Summer camp for baby cows. Vonetta rolled her eyes. Somewhere in it all, Vonetta and I suspected that JimmyTrotter hadn't told the whole truth, which Fern was better off not knowing.

"I milk Sophie every morning. About four thirty. Sometimes five. I milk her again around four when I get home from school. Well, school's out for now, so I don't have to worry about rushing."

"Twice every day?" I asked.

"That's what I said."

"Yeah," Vonetta said. "Didn't you catch that?"

I paid Vonetta no mind. I couldn't believe my cousin had to milk a cow twice a day, every day.

I bent down and touched one of Sophie's fat udders. The low-hanging balloon looked like it could burst any minute, it was so full. Vonetta and Fern went, "Eww."

"What if you miss a day?" I asked.

"Can't miss a day."

"What do you mean, you can't miss a day? What would happen if you did?"

"Why do you have to know?" Vonetta asked. "If he can't miss a day of milking that cow, he can't miss a day."

"I asked him, not you."

JimmyTrotter shook his head like he was beyond our

squabbling. "I can't miss a day. Cow's gotta get milked. I gotta be here to milk her. Just think about storing up all that milk. How much that'd hurt. She can't milk herself, Delphine."

"Oh," Fern said. "Poor Sophie."

Vonetta rolled her eyes and sighed.

"So you can't go out for track or baseball?" I asked.

"It's football around here, cuz," he said. "Or for me, the sky club. And no."

"Sky club?" Vonetta asked. "What's that?"

"For kids who want to fly. Or like airplanes." He tried to be cool but he smiled too much to be cool.

"But what happens if you're not here to milk Sophie?" I asked.

"Miss Trotter milks her."

"Isn't she too old?" I asked. "No offense."

"No offense to me," he said. "Just don't let Miss Trotter hear you."

Fern asked, "What about Butter?"

"Butter's getting her milking gears in order. She'll be dropping that calf in a month. By then, Sophie'll start to really taper off and Butter'll be on, milking up a storm. We try to time it just right so no one's without milk. A lot of our neighbors still like it fresh, and we're a lot closer than the McDaniels' farm. But if you want cream or butter you go to the store or to McDaniels'."

"Butter? Oh, nuts!" Fern cried. She loved buttered

bread, and probably felt bad about taking one more thing from a cow.

When I watched JimmyTrotter milk Sophie three years ago, he didn't seem to like milking any more than I liked ironing white sheets in the heat. Now he'd talked himself into liking it and washed Sophie's udders and hanging milk bag like it was nothing. I didn't care what Big Ma said about being raised down here. One day he'd speak up for himself when he saw everyone else flying an airplane except him. Then we'd see how fast and plain he'd "Yes'm" Miss Trotter.

Vonetta and Fern had had enough of watching milk shoot out of Sophie. They wanted to talk to Miss Trotter, although neither could settle on what they'd call her—Aunt Miss Trotter or Great Miss Trotter.

"Holler when the milking's done and it's in a bottle," Vonetta said.

"Holler when you're done hurting poor Sophie."

"It doesn't hurt her," Vonetta said.

"That's what you think," Fern said.

JimmyTrotter looked up to see that my sisters were gone. "We don't have use for bulls but once every other year for mating." He kept his voice low. "We were hoping Sophie was carrying a female. We could sure use a young milking cow, especially with Sophie getting older. No such luck."

While JimmyTrotter milked Sophie, I told him what happened earlier with Big Ma and why she was anxious to get rid of us for the day.

"I don't see the big deal over ironing sheets," he said.

"I know you don't and I can't explain it. I just didn't want to be ironing and sweating. You know what ironing and sweating is?"

"Tell me." I knew he found me silly even before I said another word.

"Ironing and sweating when you don't have to be ironing and sweating is oppression. And I won't be oppressed."

I was going for a "Right on, cuz!" but JimmyTrotter laughed. "That's oppression to you? Ironing a bedsheet and perspiring?"

"Sometimes you have to stand up for yourself."

"Sometimes you have to know when to stand up and when to iron."

"Like milking cows?" I asked.

"I don't mind milking. I don't," he said. But we didn't speak for a while. I was about to leave him with Sophie, when he said, "Delphine." There was too long a pause after he said my name. "You have a boyfriend?"

My skin must have darkened. My face certainly got warm. "I did."

"What happened? Started feeling oppressed and broke it off?"

I hated it when he laughed at me so I played it off with a shrug. "We're going to junior high in September."

"And?"

"And I might as well have broken it off. You know how it is," I said as cool as I could muster. "You get to your new school with all new people and suddenly you don't want to be stuck with the same people you've known since the third grade. It's like not growing up."

"Oh." He was smiling at me like he'd seen through me. Smiling but silently laughing, I was sure.

"So do you have a girlfriend?" I asked.

He smiled and kept milking. He intended to make me wait. Finally he said, "I had a girlfriend. Reddish-gold hair. What do they call that? Strawberry blond? Brown eyes. Freckles right here." He pointed to the bridge of my nose. "And pretty? Boy, she was pretty." He whistled. Then Sophie mooed. He took the pails of milk and set them to the side away from Sophie.

"We kept it secret and at first she understood—even said it was romantic and star-crossed. Yeah. Star-crossed. Then one day she said, 'Let's make a statement. To everyone in Autauga County. Let's hold hands so everyone can see.' I said, 'You crazy? You want to get me killed?' But she kept talking about the 'Age of Aquarius' and how we're not our parents and such. And I said no. I wouldn't walk up the school steps holding her hand for the world to see. Know what she said? She said, 'James Trotter, if you don't

80

hold my hand I'll scream so loud I'll wake your dead kin and mine.'"

"What did you do?"

"I left her there."

He was probably waiting for me to say something but I was still taking it all in. I'd never heard a story like that.

His eyes became bright in place of a smile. "Know what scorn is, cuz?"

I nodded a cool yes but I was searching my brain for the word *scorn*. I knew it wasn't good. It sounded like *scorched*. Like something burnt.

"No one wants to be made a fool of," JimmyTrotter said. "'Specially a girl. That's where scorn comes in."

I said nothing.

He laughed a little bit, although I knew he didn't think it was funny. "I locked myself in my room when I got home, waited for a knock on the door and for her family to be on the other side."

"Did they ever come?"

He shook his head. "No."

That's Entertainment

We had been gone long enough. Long enough, I hoped, for Big Ma to forget why she had us "git" to begin with. The smells of cabbage, potatoes, and meat on top of burnt cornstarch, lavender, and metal from an afternoon of ironing saluted me when I walked inside Ma Charles's house. I was hungry, and ashamed, but glad to be back. I hugged my apology to Big Ma, and for all of a second, she let me, and then she pushed me off of her, which was her way and her forgiveness. "Go on and wash up" was all she said.

We sat at the dinner table, mosquito-stung and ravenous from our hike. When Ma Charles told me to say the prayer, I asked, "Aren't we waiting for Uncle Darnell?"

Vonetta cut her eyes but kept her mouth closed.

Speaking her sassy mind was what had gotten her Big Ma's belt just before Pa had asked Big Ma to leave our home in Brooklyn. If anything, the sting of Big Ma's white church belt should have encouraged Vonetta to make that whipping her last.

"He's working an extra shift," Big Ma said. I got the feeling our uncle would be working more extra shifts now that we were here.

"Get to praying so we can get to eating!" Ma Charles said. We laughed because our great-grandmother's impatience was unexpected.

"Rolls," Big Ma said. "Delphine, go get—" Then, just as I was about to scoot out of my chair, she stopped herself, got up, and went inside the kitchen and came back with the rolls. I should have felt a victory, knowing Big Ma now thought twice about having me do everything. But I felt only shame and said the dinner prayer as fast as I could.

The "Amen" was barely out of our mouths when Ma Charles rapped on the table and said, "Well?"

"Yes, ma'am?" I asked. The South just slipped out of me. Big Ma smiled.

"Well, what did she say about my gift? Speak up," Ma Charles demanded.

I fixed my mind and mouth to say, "Nothing, really," but Vonetta jumped in front of me. "Miss Trotter said—" She made her face like our great-aunt, down to the pinched nose, and said, "Dentures? Dentures?" Then she opened her mouth full of cabbage and beef to show teeth and mimicked Miss Trotter's strong and high-pitched voice: "Go on, young'ns. Run your finger 'longside the uppers and lowers." And she chomped her teeth, even though Miss Trotter did no such thing.

I was set to kick Vonetta for repeating Miss Trotter's words and tone like that. But Ma Charles seemed to enjoy Vonetta's imitation and reared her head back and cackled. "Do it again," she said. "Just like that over-the-creek gal said it. Go on." And she readied herself to hear it as if she were waiting for the second act of the show. For her, this was entertainment.

Vonetta obliged her, only too pleased to perform. She cleared her throat. "Tell her my teeth are just fine. Tell her, why would a wolf need teeth she already has?"

Ma Charles slapped the table and cackled harder and longer. Vonetta was in her glory. "What else she say?"

Fern started to speak, but Vonetta hushed her. "This is my story. Mine." Vonetta cleared her throat again, put on her Miss Trotter face, and said, "Denture rinse. I got something for her. You wait."

Ma Charles applauded. "Go on, baby. One more time."

Big Ma had had enough. "Less talking and more eating. Good food is hard to come by."

In spite of Big Ma's order, Vonetta repeated her line. If Big Ma asked for a tree switch, I would have run out to the pecan tree and found a nice one.

"This is your fault, Delphine."

I almost choked on a gob of mashed potatoes. Big Ma's forgiveness wore off quickly.

"Marching them through the woods, across the creek to dig up trouble."

"Big Ma, you said 'Git' and they wanted to see cousin JimmyTrotter."

"And the cows," Fern added.

Ma Charles cackled. "They saw an old cow, all right."

Vonetta and Fern laughed at their great-grandmother for calling her half sister a cow. Ma Charles and Miss Trotter might as well have been Vonetta and Fern, the way they sniped at each other.

"The Lord wants you to make peace, Ma," our grandmother said. "Before the sweet by-and-by."

Ma Charles coughed or rolled her eyes or made a sound that was as good as teeth sucking. "I'll make peace when that old Negro Injun makes peace first." To Vonetta she added, "And you can tell her I said so."

Part-time Indian

Since Vonetta wanted to ride JimmyTrotter's bike and Fern wanted to moo with Sophie and Butter, we spent most of our days with JimmyTrotter and his great-grandmother. Whenever we came across the creek, Vonetta wheeled JimmyTrotter's bicycle out of the barn and rode it in circles around the barn and house while Fern chased after her. JimmyTrotter and I always lagged behind to talk about teenage things while keeping an eye on Vonetta and Fern.

"You catching on?" JimmyTrotter asked with a smirk.

"I got it," I told him. "But why?"

He shrugged. "It's how they want it. Now that you and your sisters are here, you can play along while I get back to my airplane models." He told me the story that I had heard pieces of from Pa. The story Big Ma didn't want spoken aloud. How my great-great-grandfather, Slim Jim Trotter, married two women at the same time.

"How do you know this?" I asked.

"'Cause I hear it every third day. Milk the cow, cross the creek to Aunt Naomi, and she tells me her side. Then I come back home to Miss Trotter with a basketful of eggs, and as she inspects each dozen, hoping for a bad egg to fuss about, she tells her side. I know the story inside and out. Backward and forward."

"Don't you get tired of hearing it?"

"What do you think, cousin?" He kicked a cone in his path. "I won't be around long. When I go off to flight school who'll they tell?"

"Why don't they just tell each other? They seem to be the only ones interested."

"They don't speak to each other."

"Never?"

JimmyTrotter thought for a second. "Only once that I recall."

"Oh." I knew when. The funerals. Four caskets.

"Auntie said, 'Sorry for your losses, Ruth.' Then Miss Trotter said, 'Thank you kindly, Naomi.' Then your grandmother invited us in for the repast but Miss Trotter said she wasn't up to it and we went home."

It was funny that Big Ma loved her soap operas during the day, television dramas at night, and supermarket gossip magazines when Uncle Darnell brought them in for her, but she wouldn't talk about our own family.

"Our family is a regular nighttime soap opera."

"You got that right," JimmyTrotter said.

We had a nice lunch and a slice of pie that came in a white bakery box. Unlike Ma Charles, Miss Trotter sent Jimmy-Trotter into town to buy groceries from the store. She kept an herb garden for her "medicinals," as she called them, and a much smaller vegetable garden than Ma Charles's, but she had no hard, fast rules about where everything came from. She chose to be stubborn in other ways.

Miss Trotter watched us gobble down the pie, her own cheeks rising in little, hard apples. Then she asked us, "Speak up if you know who Augustus is."

Fern said, "I don't know who it is, but I know when it is."

"Not August, dope," Vonetta said.

"Cut it out, Vonetta," I said.

"Can't one of my sister's prized greats tell us who Augustus is?"

We didn't know who Augustus was, which suited Miss Trotter just fine, and that was the point.

"Earliest we know, we sprung from my grandfather, Augustus," Miss Trotter began, but not without a few words of spite disguised as pity about Ma Charles. "She didn't bother to tell you that? Well, maybe she's getting on and can't remember the family history. Poor old thing."

JimmyTrotter tossed me a wink.

"I was going to mix up something special to repay her for the denture rinse but I'll give you some history instead." To Vonetta she said, "Tell her, 'Great-granny, today we learned our family history from one who knows it.' That'll repay her just fine."

Vonetta promised she'd say it just like that, even with me balling my fist at her.

"Our Augustus, my daddy's daddy, was not a free man, but became one: a freedman. He wasn't a man at all. Just more than a boy. Like this'n." Her chin pointed to JimmyTrotter. "Only younger."

Miss Trotter was all too happy to tell the history and to have someone to tell it to. I knew she had told this story over and over because she sang it more than she plain-spoke it. She said, "One night when the cotton was ready for picking, Augustus looked at his hands and they bled. Just bled at the thought of having to pick cotton from daybreak to day-be-done. 'No more bleeding and picking cotton for me,' he said. So Augustus watched the moon and stars in the pitch of night and chose his time and stole away. Through the woods. And the marshes. And prickly burs and such. He grew hungry shortly after he'd set out and came upon a lake. In that freshwater lake, fish with long whiskers swam down deep and close to the mud. He knew this and knelt and raised his stick to spear one, but the fish slipped on by. He tried again and missed. And missed again. When he was mad enough to spit, the water laughed at him. Augustus didn't like the water laughing at him so he said, 'Stop your laughing at me.'"

Miss Trotter raised her make-believe spear for my sisters' delight, thrusting it downward, and Fern gasped, which Miss Trotter liked.

"He felt something smack the side of his face. It seemed that laughing catfish's tail jumped up and splashed him. Augustus was fit to be tied. He was hungry and that catfish was making sport of him, so Augustus bided his time. He studied the ripple of the water, studied his fish wriggling this way and that, found the spot where the ripple and wriggling flowed as one, and speared that rascal with the sharp end of his stick. Just when Augustus knew he'd humbled that rascal, he heard the laughter again! But the laughter didn't come from the water. It came from behind him. When he turned, he saw eyes that belonged to a girl, no taller than he. She led him to her family, who'd fished those creeks since the creeks ran. When he came into their family to live as one of them, the girl's father said his daughter had caught a big, black fish. He told his daughter she increased their wealth and when the time came and she was old enough, she could claim her prize.

"It wasn't long until all the Indians that lived along the creek, the pine, and the coast were forced to move themselves from the land and go west until their feet bled and the old folks dropped. Isn't it funny that even the good things of the earth can make your hands and feet bleed? And that is as far back as we know. Back to my father's father. A boy named Augustus. Now, take that back with you."

As soon as we were on our way, Vonetta said, "We're Indians. Just like Great Miss Trotter."

"Aunt Miss Trotter," Fern said. "JimmyTrotter has aunts. We have one too."

"I guess that makes us part Indian," I said. "Just part." But I already knew this from looking at Slim Jim Trotter standing next to my great-great-grandmother Livonia.

"My part's probably bigger than yours. I look more like Miss Trotter than you do."

"That's silly, Vonetta," I said. "You, Fern, and I are all the same. From Pa and Cecile. We're what they are. Black."

"And Afro-American without the Afros."

"If you know so much, why is our grandpa Indian and we're not?"

"Great-great-grandfather," I told her. "And if you were listening with your ears you'd know he was half Indian." I spoke with my foot all in it although I wasn't sure.

"Still Indian," she both sulked and insisted.

"Vonetta, I thought you were good at math," I said.

"You thought right." I let the sass slide because I was making a point and didn't want to get sidetracked.

"If both ours and JimmyTrotter's great-great-grandmas were black, and our great-great-grandpa was half Indian, I repeat, *half . . .*"

She cut her eyes at me and sucked her teeth but again, I let it slide and continued, ". . . half Indian and half black, then Ma Charles and Miss Trotter are what?"

"Sisters," she said.

Vonetta had cooked up in her head that she was Pocahontas now that we'd heard the story of Augustus joining into his Indian family.

I sucked my teeth hard. "I can't believe you, Vonetta. You know your fractions. You know better."

Vonetta sucked her teeth extra hard back.

"Look," I said. "We come from the Gaither side too. We're what they are."

"Black and proud," Fern said.

"We come from the Charles side and we're what they are."

"Colored," Fern said, because Big Ma preferred to be called "colored."

"We come from the Johnson side from Cecile and we're what they are."

Fern said, "Far, far away."

"Stack up all the black parts, next to the Indian part—"

Fern said, "And you got a whole pie."

"I don't care what you say," Vonetta said. "I'm still part Indian."

How I Met My Sister

Vonetta did what Miss Trotter wanted. She repaid Ma Charles in full. Instead of talking about helping with the cows or having apple pie, Vonetta recited a small bit of our newly learned family history. She made sure she began her recitation with that mean thing Miss Trotter coached her to say: "Great-granny, today we learned our family history from one who knows it." Once Vonetta began performing the history, not even the threat of a whipping from Big Ma could stop her, especially with Ma Charles egging her on.

"Is that what that Negro Injun told you?" Ma Charles said. Her twinkling eyes told on her. Ma Charles was more entertained than she was indignant.

"Why do you call her that?" I asked. "She's your sister."

"That's none of your business," Big Ma said.

"Sister," Ma Charles said, and now she was indignant. "I didn't know I had one until the first day of school. I went to Miss Rice's classroom because that's where all the coloreds went to learn how to read, write, and not be cheated at the store in town. Picture all of us in one classroom. A handful of kids. Big, small. Dark. Brown. Yellow. Ages five to fifteen. First day of school Miss Rice said to me, 'Go on, take the seat next to your sister.' I said as nice as I could, 'I have no sister, Miss Rice.' Then she said, 'Child, go sit down next to Ruthie Trotter, the girl with your face and name. Go on.'"

"That's how you met your own sister?" Fern asked.

"All the colored folk on both sides of the creek knew. No one bothered to tell me."

"She's still your sister," I said. "Aren't you whatever she is?"

Big Ma planted her hand on the table and searched upward. "A mercy, Lord. A mercy at the dinner table."

"And that makes us Indians too, right?" Vonetta hoped more than asked.

"When the census came around, my mama told them to put 'colored' for our household. She was so dark they put 'Negro,' because black was the only color they saw in her. Even though Miss Ella Pearl, Miss Trotter's mother, was as colored as my mother, she told the census taker to write 'Indian.'" Ma Charles laughed a *heh-heh-heh*. "Next time you go to see the old cows, ask Miss Trotter which fountain she drinks out of when she goes to town."

"Now, now, Ma. They took those signs down years ago."

Ma Charles ignored her. "This is better than the Lone Ranger and Tonto. Go ahead, young'n. Say it again. Leave nothing out."

Talk about spinning straw. Suddenly, the little bit of family history Vonetta had first recited spun itself into a long, winding yarn. Vonetta was only too happy to transform her face and her voice into Miss Trotter's to retell the story of our oldest known ancestor, Augustus the runaway. She found Miss Trotter's storytelling rhythm, turned her fingers into stars, and thrust her spear into the water. She didn't spare a single detail as she told how his hands bled and he looked up to those stars and ran away until he got hungry and the water laughed and splashed his face, and when he reached to get the fish he felt two eyes on him. And that was how he found the Indian girl who brought him to her people and they became one rich, happy family and moved west together.

Ma Charles asked for her tambourine.

Fern applauded.

Big Ma was disgusted.

Even though Ma Charles was thoroughly entertained, she said, "Don't let her tell those stories about her people. How they brought my grandfather into the tribe as one of their own. When she tells that story be respectful because that is my handiwork in you."

To that, Big Ma said, "*Your* handiwork in *my* grandkids? It's all I can do to wash and wring the Brooklyn and Oakland out of them and keep them good proper Negroes—"

Then Fern said, "Black and proud," and Big Ma said, "Eat your food."

Ma Charles agreed. "Eat your food, Rickets"—her new name for Fern because she wouldn't eat the food that puts meat on bones—"and you," she said to Vonetta, "nod and say, 'Yes ma'am, Miss Trotter,' because she likes to hear that. Miss Trotter. The Lord knows she paid everything she got to be called Miss Trotter, so call her that. But you're old enough to know the truth, daughter."

I figured when Ma Charles didn't have a name handy, she called any woman or girl younger than herself "daughter."

"You're old enough, and since we are telling it, we will tell it all."

"A mercy, Lord."

"They took in my grandfather, a runaway from the cotton fields. He was about ten. At that time, there was trouble down in Eufaula. War with the last of the Creek. She didn't tell you this part of the history, did she? Hmph. When the last of them was defeated, the governor made the Indians march west to Oklahoma and Texas, and Augustus marched with them. He married the Indian girl, all right, according to their ways when he became a man. Sixteen. Seventeen. She bore eleven of his children over twenty years. Some look more Indian. Some look more colored. Each time one was born, her father said, 'See how my daughter increases our wealth?' Hmp." Ma Charles spat in the house without anything coming out and Big Ma called for a mercy. "My father was the second to the last boy. Don't let her tell you how Indian he was— he looked just as colored as his pa.

"Quiet as it's kept, Indians got good money for their colored. Good money. There came a time when my grand-mother's brothers sold my grandfather and four of his colored children into the very cotton fields he freed him-self from."

"Can they do that?" I asked.

"What do they teach you in school?" she asked. "They did that. This is history I'm telling you. The real history she won't tell you."

"Indians wouldn't do that," I said. "The Indians were oppressed like us. They wouldn't collaborate with the Man."

Big Ma said, "Delphine, I know your father spoke to you girls about using that Black Panther language down here."

"He surely did, Big Ma."

"I know he did," Big Ma said to Fern. "Because he doesn't want me to have to ship you back to him in a pine box."

97

At the moment I didn't care about what Pa told us. I couldn't believe what Ma Charles said about the Indians. I wouldn't believe it. "They sold black people?"

She nodded like this was common knowledge. "Sold some. Kept some. The woolly-haired colored ones were the first to go. I know it because my father done seen it with his own eyes. Seen his father tied up like a mule and his sisters and brothers led away. Seen it when he was but ten or eleven. His mother hid him because his hair was more wool than straight. But he still had seen it all. How his mother fell to the ground begging her brothers and uncles. So when she tells you they were a happy clan, say, 'Yes, ma'am, Miss Trotter,' like I showed you how. Don't call her a liar to her face. The Lord doesn't love a disrespectful child. She is old and she is kin. But I am equal to her in years. I pulled her pigtails in Miss Rice's classroom. I can call her a liar, but don't you do it. Do like I told you. Say, 'Yes ma'am, Miss Trotter.' She likes the sound of that. 'Miss Trotter.'" Then she said it again. "Lord knows she paid enough to be called that. Miss Trotter."

Little Miss Ethel Waters

The next day while we were hiking across the field, through the pines, and over the creek to see JimmyTrotter, Miss Trotter, and the cows, I told Vonetta, "Don't tell her everything Ma Charles said."

Vonetta said, "You can't tell me what to say. You can't control me."

"Come in, mission control," Fern said in her walkie-talkie voice, then used another voice to say, "This is mission control, over."

Vonetta told her to shut up and I told Vonetta to shut up. Then Vonetta took a swat at Fern and missed, then I took a swat at Vonetta and didn't miss. "So there," I said.

"I hate you, Delphine." She rubbed her shoulder.

"I don't care, Vonetta."

Fern didn't seem to need my protection. She ignored Vonetta and kept on saying, "This is control. We have control. Over."

I said to Vonetta, "Ma Charles is just telling us like it was. That doesn't mean she wants you to repeat everything she says."

"How do you know?" Vonetta said.

Fern, suddenly back from playing "mission control," said in Ma Charles's voice, "Don't *you* call her a liar." She pointed at Vonetta. "You, you, you."

"That's right," I said, glad Fern paid attention, both now and last night. "Ma Charles said *she* could call Miss Trotter a liar—"

"But don't *you* do it," Fern said, clunking her turtle head. "Don't you do it."

"I'm not even going to talk to Miss Trotter," Vonetta said. "I'm going to ride JimmyTrotter's bike because I'm good at it."

"And I'm going to moo with the cows. Check out what's on their minds," Fern said.

And that was fine with me.

This time we walked farther down to the shallower end of the creek and wriggled out of our sneakers to wade across. It took longer to reach our great-aunt and cousin but we needed to cool down. Once we made it over the creek and ran through the pines, Vonetta was galloping to the house looking for Miss Trotter. I knew she was going to tell it and I couldn't stop her. Miss Trotter was eager for every word.

"Is that what she told you?" Miss Trotter said. "I'd have pulled her pigtails too, if she had enough to pull." My great-aunt was no better than Vonetta. She only sought to have something mean to say about Ma Charles when she and her sister had the same type, color, and length of hair.

When she was done being snippy, Miss Trotter said, "I can't fault her. No sir." Then I felt badly for thinking the worst of Miss Trotter now that her tone had changed. "Can't say I blame her at all."

I grabbed on to the sorrow in her voice it like it was hope. Maybe for once our great-grandmothers would stop acting like Vonetta and Fern and behave like sisters.

"It's not her fault she had no father to tell her about the family. The history. How could she know what is true? How could she know our father?" Then she said to Vonetta, in a voice so sweet I almost believed her, "But dear one, don't tell her she grew up with no father. No, no. Don't you tell her that. Don't tell her how our father's boots stood outside this very porch before he came in to supper. My mother kept a clean house, so Papa's boots had to stay out on the porch. I remember clearly, but my poor sister had no fine, happy memories of a father coming home to tuck her in or tell her stories. How can she tell you the right and true history if she doesn't know it? Poor sister. Dear sister."

I was disappointed. I almost believed her pity. I saw through her, but Fern and Vonetta were reeled in. "Poor sister," Fern cooed.

"I have all my remembrances of him and how he loved *my* mama," she crowed. And then she began to story-talk. "My father walked on land like a man who could walk on all the elements. Land. Air. Water. He was good with the coloreds and good with the whites. He was good with the men, and the women thought he was mighty fine. When he was a boy among his people, he'd wave to the trains passing through the reservation. Wave and wave. When he got to be about JimmyTrotter's age, maybe older, a man from the railroad went to the Indian Affairs agent and got my papa a pass to work on the railroads. Those same railroads you pass along the way. My papa was long-limbed and scrawny, but he worked hard and caused no trouble. They let him work on the Montgomery and West Point train. He loved his trains. All the railroad companies wanted a worker as fine and hardworking as Slim Jim Trotter. He was what they saw: The coloreds called him a good man, slim as a rail. The whites called him a good Injun. They gave him the hardest work but that didn't stop Papa, no sir! He worked his way from being on the section gang repairing railroad track, and then he became a fireman shoveling coal on the freight train. Train always stopped in Autauga County, where cotton, the lumber mills, and textile mills were king. Papa rode with the trains. The work was good. He was always gone."

At this point JimmyTrotter slipped away and left us with Miss Trotter. He'd been hearing these stories for years.

"The prettiest sight my papa ever seen was my mama, Miss Ella Pearl, gathering white potato vine. He loved her from the start, brought her to the courthouse in town and married her, and she became his legal wife.

"But don't let on you know your great-granny's shame," Miss Trotter said. "Don't hurt an old woman with the truth. No, no, dear one," she told Vonetta. "Don't let on you know."

I wouldn't let my sister carry half-true histories back and forth between Miss Trotter and her sister. I said, "Aunt Ruth," because that was her name. Ruth Trotter.

"Great Miss Trotter was all I agreed to."

"Great Miss Trotter," I said. "Vonetta can't repeat all of that. I won't let her."

"You can't make me do anything. I'm liberated," Vonetta said. "It's up to me to tell or not tell."

"That's right," Miss Trotter agreed. "That's up to you to don't tell, like I said, not to tell." Even with all of that "don't telling," Miss Trotter was egging Vonetta on to tell.

"That's right," Vonetta said.

"That's right, dear one," Miss Trotter said. And Vonetta

rolled around in that "dear one" name like it was a pink rabbit-fur jacket.

Since Vonetta couldn't see she was a bouncing ball being played between the two sisters, I knew I had to do what Pa and Cecile wanted me to do. I had to look out for her.

So I asked Miss Trotter, "Why can't you go and see your sister, Aunt Miss Trotter? Why can't you talk to her?"

"She's the one who must beg my pardon. She must walk to my home."

"But she's the only sister you have."

"She's the only one I know about."

"That's why you should see her."

"Before the sweet by-and-by," Fern added.

For a second Miss Trotter's pride fell from her face. Then it found its way back to her eyes, cheeks, and mouth. "We all have to go sometime. It's the way of things."

As sure as Miss Trotter counted on Vonetta to be showy, crowy, and unstoppable, Vonetta couldn't wait until Ma Charles said, "Well?" Vonetta couldn't get the story out fast enough, throwing in every pause, hand motion, and "No sir!"

"Is that what she told you?" Ma Charles said.

" 'He loved her from the start, brought her to the courthouse in town and married her, and she became his legal wife.' " It was the one of the few phrases that Vonetta got word for word.

"Truth is, the train stopped in Prattville proper. But Papa didn't like town so much and he roamed the country until it was time to pick up on the train again. My papa, Slim Jim Trotter, found my mother on her way to teach Bible school. My mother, your great-great-grandmother, said, 'The Lord put this man in my path, so I married him in the church of God.'"

Then she said to Vonetta, "Let me see how you're going to tell it. Go on, little Miss Ethel Waters. Let's see."

I had seen enough old movies to know Ethel Waters was an old-time actress in the black-and-white pictures. Vonetta didn't know who she was but that didn't stop her from reciting, "The good Lord put this man . . ."

By the time Big Ma had come out of her room to see what all the commotion and cackling was about, it was too late. Vonetta already had her instructions for the next day's performance.

"Well, I have heard enough of it," Big Ma said. "Your father sent you down here to play checkers and read a book. Not to stir up stuff."

Ma Charles said, "If they want to milk cows and fill up on silly half-Indian tales, let 'em go."

Vonetta and Fern hollered, "YAY!" and Big Ma told them to stop gobbling like wild turkeys at a Thanksgiving turkey shoot. That only encouraged them to gobble and strut around, and Ma Charles got a big kick out of that.

"All they're doing is getting your pressure up. That's

right. They'll leave me motherless when your pressure flies sky high."

"Off to the sweet by-and-by," Fern sang.

Only Big Ma's pressure went up. Ma Charles was enjoying the evening performances.

"But if you marry Mr. Lucas, you won't be lonely and you'll have peach cobbler every Sunday," Fern said.

"Even Rickets knows the truth!" Ma Charles hollered.

But just to make sure the attention didn't stray too far from her, Vonetta became Little Miss Ethel Waters and practiced the next day's retelling for Ma Charles.

Every Sprig

It rained so heavily over the next two days, we stayed at Ma Charles's and played Old Maid. When the sky's color returned to clear blue and the air was once again clean-smelling, we ran outside and let the chickens out of the coop, and between us and Caleb, we kept an eye on them so they wouldn't get away. Big Ma had me help her clip their wing feathers, which neither the chickens nor Fern appreciated, but clipping their wings made it easier to keep track of them while they strutted about the yard. When they had enough freedom, we chased them inside the run, where they could still strut about freely.

The next day we went back over to Miss Trotter's, happy to have the walk and to wade down at the shallow end of the creek. After we had our fill of being on the other side, I told Miss Trotter, "I don't understand why you can't talk to your sister face-to-face, Miss Trotter."

"Respect your elders, Delphine," Vonetta said. "Great Miss Trotter can do what she wants."

"You tell her," Great Miss Trotter said.

"Well, she is eld," Fern pointed out to me. "Past tense for old."

Miss Trotter said, "She's the one who must come this way and beg my pardon. She has to walk to my home and wipe clean that hex she put over my generations."

"Hex?" I asked.

"It means bad luck," Vonetta said.

"I know what it means," I snapped at her. She was only brave because Miss Trotter was right there.

Miss Trotter said, "My sister has done many a wicked thing against me out of envy. Many a wicked thing."

"Ma Charles?" I asked. "Our great-grandmother?"

"She wasn't born a great-granny," Miss Trotter said. "She was a young, wicked, jealous girl. When Steven Hazzard courted and married me, she married Henry Charles to keep up with me. My husband understood about my father and let me keep my name and let me name our son after my father. But the wicked one couldn't let that be. One Sunday as we strolled in town, she on one side of the street with her husband, and me with mine and my son in arms, she said, 'Well, if it isn't the Trotters. Hiya, Steven Trotter.' That was the last I seen of my husband."

Miss Trotter didn't strike me to be a crying woman, but I saw her tears well up although she wouldn't let them roll. She pointed her finger at me and said, "She wiped out every sprig of my generations—she hates me so. Wiped out each one but JimmyTrotter."

"Ma Charles didn't do any such thing. She wouldn't." As I held my stare with Miss Trotter I knew it didn't matter that I didn't believe in hexes or curses. My great-aunt did, and for that matter, so did my great-grandmother.

Miss Trotter turned to Vonetta and put on her sweet voice. "What was that you told your sister?"

Vonetta knew when she was being coached and ate it up. "I told her to respect her elders."

"That's right! Respect!" Miss Trotter cried out. "You!"—she went from sweetness to pointing and almost shouting at me—"haven't lived as long as my toenails! You don't know what Naomi did and didn't do. Would or wouldn't do. Now, if she has something to say to me, she can journey over the creek on her two feet. Her two feet." She turned to Vonetta, her helpmate. "Go get that cane, dear one."

Vonetta took off like a foot soldier in Miss Trotter's army. She returned with the wooden cane, presenting it with pride to her general.

"Yes, yes," Miss Trotter said, and kissed Vonetta on her

forehead. We weren't a kissing kind of family, so Vonetta ate that right up. "She can borrow the cane she gave me to come beg my pardon."

When we got to the house I asked my great-grandmother, "Why won't you talk to your sister?"

My great-grandmother said, "I talk to her every day."

"How is that?"

"Through prayer. I pray to the Lord for my half sister's wicked soul." But Ma Charles wasn't joking with me. There was no winking or twinkle in her eyes.

Vonetta said, "Don't worry, Ma Charles. I didn't believe the part about you chasing her husband out of town."

Ma Charles just laughed and laughed. "You tell the widow Hazzard I'm sorry for her loss." She laughed some more.

"Cut it out, Vonetta," I warned. "If you're not going to say it right you shouldn't say it at all."

"Oh, hush," Ma Charles said, eager for more. "What else she say?"

"Know what she said, Ma Charles?" Vonetta asked.

I kicked Vonetta, a really good one. Then Ma Charles said, "Don't let me see you do that again." And Vonetta moved closer to Ma Charles and rubbed the side of her leg.

"Now, what did the old cow say?"

"I'm not calling her an old cow, but Miss Trotter said if

you want to talk to her face-to-face, you have to walk on your two left feet over the creek with the cane and take the hex off her first." Vonetta added the part about "left" feet to stir up trouble. It worked.

Ma Charles leaped out of her chair—and she was generally slow-moving. "Oh! Oh! Spare her, Lord! Spare her, Lord! For I surely will get her! I surely will! Where's my tambourine?"

Big Ma came running. "Mama, Mama! Mama, sit down! Sit down, Mama!" She turned to me. "Delphine, what did you do? What did you—"

Before I knew it, my grandmother backhanded me across the cheek so hard I saw white.

I stayed away from everyone for the next day and night. I stayed up in the pecan tree with my book when I could and slept on the porch at night. Since I had already run through the other two books I had packed, I had no choice but to finish *Things Fall Apart*. It was the perfect book, since Okonkwo couldn't do right, and neither could any of the adults on this side of the creek or the other.

When I finally came down from my tree I went to Little Miss Ethel Waters first.

"Vonetta. You have to stop going back and forth telling those tales."

"I'm not telling tales and you can't tell me what to do."

I wanted to hit her right then and there. If only Cecile could see her precious Vonetta now. "Watch out for Vonetta" my fat fanny.

"Our aunt and our great-grandma should be rocking on this porch together. Not sending poison pen letters back and forth through you."

"So."

"They're old, Vonetta. And one of them is going to die first." I refused to say it the southern hymn way—"the sweet by-and-by." "Then the one left alive will say, 'I miss my sister.' And you'll feel rotten in your rotten little heart because you helped to keep them apart. Then what?"

"Yeah, then what?" Fern asked.

Vonetta crossed her arms. "One thing's for sure. I'll never miss you."

"Oh yeah? Well, I hope you don't act like this when Pa and Mrs.'s baby comes."

There was a lot of silence before there was anything else.

"What?" one asked loud.

"Baby?" The other, soft.

I didn't mean to tell them like this. It slipped out. From the looks on their faces, one trying to be proud and cool, the other crumbling, I wished I had told them sooner. And nicely.

"Pa and Mrs. are having a baby," I said. "That's why she's been so sick."

"Babies don't make you sick," Vonetta said.

"This one's making Mrs. sick," I said.

"A baby?"

"A B-A-B-Y, baby," Vonetta sang. "That means you won't be the baby, you crybaby."

"That means you won't be the middle, you show-off."

"Baby, baby, 'bout to cry. Wipe that tear from your eye."

Fern didn't bother to ball up her fists or bang them at her sides, her warning that she was about to strike. She just started to windmill-punch at Vonetta, and I let her. Vonetta whipped free and dodged to her left, then right, like a fighter in the boxing ring, taunting and teasing Fern. Vonetta was discovering her longer legs, dodging and dashing off, avoiding Fern's blows. Fern could never catch her, but I could.

"Stop picking on Fern just because you can!" I yelled at her.

"Fern's a big baby."

"And you're afraid to get your watch back, you chicken."

"I am not."

"Chicken."

"I'm not a chicken."

"You're more chicken than all those chickens in the yard—waving and smiling at those girls who are laughing at you. What do you think they call you? Certainly not Vonetta."

"I hate you, Delphine."

"I don't care. Just stop picking on Fern. She's your little sister."

Vonetta opened her mouth like she was about to say something, then shut it and walked away.

Chickweed

Vonetta and Fern didn't stay mad at each other for long. They never did. Even Vonetta and I got back to the way things were. Not completely, but enough. We didn't really talk about things.

Still, I braced myself to answer their questions about the baby, but no one asked me anything. Vonetta didn't say a word about it, but Fern went to Big Ma to ask why Pa and Mrs. needed to have a baby. Big Ma said, "Never you mind. That's your father and his wife's business," and then she sent Fern out to the coop with a pan of chicken feed. Fern mistook the chickens clamoring about her for their need to talk, so whatever she had to say about the new baby she said to the chickens.

There was nothing I could do to stop Miss Trotter from telling her history to Vonetta, or to stop Vonetta from telling Ma Charles. Even when Miss Trotter got the best of Ma Charles there was a gleam in Ma Charles's eyes when Vonetta "repaid" her with Miss Trotter's words. One sister said her father knew every flower, leaf, and root, while the other said he never messed with that stuff, but instead went to the colored doctor and dentist in town and bought penny candy for her. They might as well still be in Miss Rice's classroom pulling each other's pigtails.

The dueling between the two sisters went on and on, from one side of the creek and, thanks to Vonetta, back over to the other side of the creek. It seemed the sisters shared their father equally but they were determined to prove which one was the right and true daughter of Slim Jim Trotter. Vonetta was sure to soak up every word, every expression, to reenact later.

Miss Trotter began the latest round of family history and pigtail-pulling. "So, you see, dear one," she said sweetly, "it was her mama's fault the law went looking for my father on the charge of bigamy."

Fern's eyes popped when she heard the new word. *Bigamy.* I'd have to tell her later it wasn't the singsong word she might have imagined.

"Found him and jailed him. Took his government work

papers. They were going to send him to the Creek Nation in Oklahoma. State capital is Oklahoma City." She threw that one in like she was back in Miss Rice's classroom. "Send him back to the reservation. But first there would be a trial at the courthouse in town." She stopped to chuckle. "What they didn't know was my father walked between worlds. No jail could hold him. And he became a crow and flew between the bars and flew to me and became himself and said, 'Chickweed'—that's what he called me. 'Chickweed.'" Vonetta nodded like Miss Trotter did. "'Papa's gotta fly away. But I'll come back to you, my chickweed. I'll come back.'"

When we asked Miss Trotter if he came back she said no, and Vonetta matched her sorrow when she retold it to Ma Charles. "Never did."

"Hmp," Ma Charles said at the end of Vonetta's retelling. "Is that what she told you? Hmp."

"Ma, don't start," Big Ma said.

Ma Charles waved her away. "Hush, girl. If someone tells it, I'll tell it. I have a right."

"Right on," Fern said.

"That's right," Ma Charles agreed. "Now hear this— especially you," she said to Little Miss Ethel Waters. "My father was a God-fearing colored man. He didn't turn into a crow like some demon. No sir!"

"Ma, please," our grandmother pleaded, but Ma Charles was determined to tell her family history, so Big Ma's pleas turned to anger. "This is your doing," Big Ma said to Vonetta. To me she said, "And you keep bringing them over the creek."

I shrugged. "Nothing to do here. So we help milk the cows."

"Nothing to do?" Big Ma repeated. "Is that so? Well, I thought I'd let you have the vacation your Pa and step-mother wanted for you. There's plenty of ironing if you're bored. Teach you what wash day is all about."

But Ma Charles wanted her say and told our grand-mother to hush and gave her side of the story.

"My papa didn't turn into a crow. He knew what these colored trials were for. Entertainment! White folk would get wind of colored trials and would come into town dressed like they were going to the theater with President Lincoln and fill all the seats in the courthouse. The col-oreds were allowed to sit up in the balcony or in the back if they were a footman or maid. And the county attorney would ask questions in such a way as to encourage the colored person in the witness box to roll their eyes and shuck about and say words they didn't know the meanings of. And the judge would allow the people in the gallery to laugh a bit before banging the gavel and calling for order. They couldn't just take away my father's work pass for good and put him on a train to the Oklahoma reservation. Not a half-colored man with two colored wives. No sir! They had to bring them all in court. Have the wives make grand Negro spectacles of themselves, calling each other 'that over-the-creek woman.'

"I might not remember everything about my father, but I knew he stood taller than most men. So instead of making a mockery of my mother and me, and our holy union as a family under God, my father spared us from being the town joke. He even spared that over-the-creek woman. He waited until the sheriff went home and he unhinged the door to the jail cell with a pocket blade they didn't bother to take from him. He unlocked the front door and made his way over to us. He kissed me on the head and told me to mind my ma. And *I'm* the one he called Chickweed. Me. Not her. And that was the last I saw of him. My papa."

She took out her handkerchief from her bra and dabbed her eyes.

"See that?" Big Ma said. "No one needs to know this. You all just had to upset my mother."

We didn't hear the end of that for a week.

Still, Vonetta told Miss Trotter Ma Charles's side. Using all of Ma Charles's expressions. She even took a hankie she tied to the strap of her undershirt and cried into it.

To all that Miss Trotter said, "He called me Chickweed first."

When Ma Charles had told her side of the story, Vonetta had no pity for her own great-grandmother's tears. But when Miss Trotter's tears fell, Vonetta placed her hand to her own lips, as if to tell herself to hush, to stop carrying their tales back and forth. I didn't see it often, but I recognized a true look of sorrow and regret on my sister's face, and for that alone, I was glad.

Going to Town

When Sophie gave all that she had for the afternoon, JimmyTrotter said, "Let's make a run to town to deliver the milk. Last stop will be Aunt Naomi's and her two quarts."

"That's right," Vonetta crowed. "My milk for my cornflakes."

"*Our* cornflakes," Fern said. "As long as it's all right with Sophie, it's all right with me."

"You can drive a car, cousin?" I asked. I couldn't hide my awe and envy.

"Do you see a subway train around here?"

Vonetta and Fern screamed their excitement about going into town. We hadn't seen anything but pine trees, a bloodhound, chickens, and two cows. Even the kick we got out of having our own pecan tree or gathering peaches and lemons from Mr. Lucas's trees waned after a short while.

"I guess it's okay," I said. "Let me call Big Ma to let her know we're going."

"She knows you're with me," he said in that easy way of his, "and that's as good as her knowing. Come on, girl. Let's load up and hop in the chariot."

I knew better than to not call my grandmother but I was tired of being a killjoy, and my sisters and I were back in step with one another. We helped JimmyTrotter fill his crates with the quart bottles and he and I lugged them to the station wagon.

"We're gone to town," he called out to Miss Trotter.

She waved and said, "Then get going. If you call that gone."

"We'll circle around," JimmyTrotter said as we pulled away from Miss Trotter's. "First we'll drop off at the Prestons', the Owenses', the Browns', and the Newells'. Then we'll hit town and deliver to the grocery store, the bakery, and then last stop, Aunt Naomi." It always took a second to remember his aunt Naomi was my Ma Charles, but we cheered the delivery route like we knew where we were going.

Town wasn't a whole lot of town, but as long as there was a candy store it was town enough. We found everything we'd been missing. Candy, Royal Crown Cola, potato chips, comic books, and magazines. I was just glad for the change in scenery.

JimmyTrotter tucked the bills in his wallet after making his deliveries. Not everyone paid him, but most of his customers did, like the grocery store owner and the bakery. He explained that he wasn't their main milk supplier, but the bakery used only family-farmed milk and the grocery store still had a few customers like Ma Charles, who didn't trust big dairy farms. They gladly paid for what they could get from family farmers like the Trotters.

"I suppose Miss Trotter wouldn't mind if I treated you all to—" Vonetta and Fern screamed before he could get it out.

"Calm down," I told them, although I was thrilled at the possibility of talking my cousin into treating me to a magazine.

JimmyTrotter smirked. "Brooklyn girls. Act like you all never been off the farm."

We strolled down to the candy store, arm-in-arm-in-arm. My sisters and I broke our arm link apart to let the man with his dog coming toward us pass, but he didn't. The white man whose tan shirt had a star fixed on its pocket stood in front of JimmyTrotter and us and didn't move. His hat was like a cowboy hat with the same star pinned smack in the center.

"Good afternoon, Sheriff," JimmyTrotter said. The girls parroted him, but I said nothing.

The white man, the sheriff, looked straight at Jimmy-Trotter. He didn't return his easy smile. "Boy, what did I tell you about driving that wagon into town without a license?"

My cousin stiffened under the sheriff's questions and rebuke and could only say, "Sorry, Sheriff Charles."

"If you were sorry you wouldn't be driving that vehicle down my roads until you turned sixteen."

"Yes, sir, Sheriff Charles."

"Charles?" Vonetta asked. "Isn't that—"

I gave her a quick "Hush," and she sucked her teeth at me.

Fern was busy petting and hugging the bloodhound. He seemed to like it.

"Get from that dog," the sheriff told her. "That vicious attack dog'll chew you up and swallow you whole."

But Fern didn't move from the dog.

"Didn't you hear me? That dog's trained to attack Negroes. Now get from that dog."

The dog looked up to Fern with eyes as sad and droopy as Caleb's and panted for more love. I pulled Fern away from the sheriff's dog. As sure as I looked up at that man's face, I knew I had better.

The sheriff turned his attention back to JimmyTrotter. "You drive that vehicle back, son. But don't let me find you behind the wheel till you're sixteen and got a card in your wallet."

"Yes, sir, Sheriff Charles."

"And don't you be sneaking around driving at night, son. Lots of things happen at night to Negroes you don't want to know about."

"Yes, sir, Sheriff Charles."

"You driving that vehicle day or night, you already breaking the law. Nothing I can do for you if you break the law."

"Yes, sir, Sheriff Charles."

Each time JimmyTrotter said "Yes, sir," I felt my scalp baking. I heard Papa telling me to mind my mouth. I did what Papa said but I only grew hotter inside. The sheriff eyed me good and hard, probably knowing I was struggling to keep it in.

When the sheriff let us by, the girls still wanted their comic books and candy but I wouldn't take anything from JimmyTrotter. If I asked him for *Seventeen* magazine, I'd have to keep silent about the sheriff, and I had things to say. On the ride back I decided that I'd stayed silent long enough.

"Why'd you let the Man oppress you?"

"Oppress me?" JimmyTrotter laughed, finding his old self.

" 'Yes, sir, Sheriff Charles.' "

" 'No, sir, Sheriff Charles,' " my sisters joined in.

If JimmyTrotter was embarrassed he didn't let on. He just said, "Sheriff Charles is the law."

"The people are the law," I said.

"Power to the people," they chorused.

We hit a bump. JimmyTrotter tossed his head back and laughed. "Aunt Ophelia told me about you all flying out to Oakland to be with that Cecile woman."

"Our mother," I said.

"And a poet," Fern added.

Vonetta cleared her throat. "A black revolutionary poet."

"Auntie told me all about it," JimmyTrotter went on. "She said that Cecile got you all mixed up with the Black Panthers." He laughed some more.

"Best summer of our lives was at the People's Center," I said.

"Better if we went to Disneyland like we were supposed to," Vonetta said.

"Even better if we shook hands with Mickey and Minnie."

"Well, keep making a fist and shouting 'Power to the people!' around here. Keep it up," he warned.

I heard how JimmyTrotter meant it but Vonetta and Fern didn't. They did what they heard and raised their fists and shouted "Power to the people!" and "Seize the time!" and "Right on!"

When we were done being loud and revolutionary we

asked JimmyTrotter about the sheriff.

"Why does he have the same name as Ma Charles?"

"And the same dog?"

"And now that I think of it," Vonetta said, "the same eyes as Big Ma."

"That's your blood cousin," JimmyTrotter said. "Yours. Not mine."

"That white man?" Vonetta asked.

"And his dog?" Fern asked.

I felt my cousin once again standing over me. Knowing more than I knew. We drove along.

"Ma Charles's husband—your great-grandpa Henry—was kin to Sheriff Charles."

"Ma Charles married a white man?" Vonetta asked. I would have asked the same question but Vonetta was awfully quick these days. Either that, or I at least thought before letting stuff fly out of my mouth.

"Not Uncle Henry," he said. "His daddy's father, Rufus Charles. Back then, *Master* Rufus Charles." He said it like, *Don't yawl know anything?* "The Charles family owned a good deal of the cotton around here, way back then. And the slaves."

"And the slaves? Like his own son? How can you own a member of your family?" I said. "That's just wrong."

"Calm down, cuz," JimmyTrotter said. "It's just history. Or don't they teach that in Brooklyn?"

"Down with slavery," I said, my fist in the air.

127

"Get down, slavery. Get down and stay down," Vonetta agreed.

Fern pointed her finger as if she was commanding a dog. "Heel, slavery!"

JimmyTrotter shook his head like we were ignorant lunatics. "You know slavery's been over a hundred years, cuz."

I could see Vonetta counting backward in her head and on her fingers. "One hundred and four years."

"Didn't seem like it to me," I sang back. "*Yes, sir, Master Charles. No, sir, Master Charles.*"

After no one said anything, Vonetta broke the silence. "So we're white too?"

When we neared Ma Charles's house, Caleb was already making a ruckus. Big Ma came outside and scolded him to hush, probably because she didn't want Elijah Lucas to step out on his porch. Fern was the first to jump out of the station wagon. She raced over to Caleb, who sniffed and licked all over her and sang his sad dog song. She threw her arms around his neck and sang with him.

JimmyTrotter gave Vonetta one of the last two milk bottles and told her not to drop it. I had the other bottle.

"Are you kidding me?" she sassed. "I'm going to have a bowl of cornflakes with milk as soon as I get inside!" Vonetta said. If she cared as much about hurting Fern's feelings or finding her missing watch as she cared for a bowl of cereal swimming in milk, most of her problems would be solved.

To Big Ma's consternation, Mr. Lucas stepped out on his porch and called out, "Ophelia! Ophelia!" like her name was a song. Big Ma didn't wave to him. She waved him off, like, *Stop that!* I don't think it made a difference to Mr. Lucas.

"Don't know why he makes a big noise of himself."

"Caleb?" Fern asked.

Big Ma seemed mad, embarrassed, and tickled all at once. She said, "Um-hmm," but I knew she wasn't talking about the bloodhound.

Aunt Jemima, Who?

Once we learned that our great-great-grandfather on the Charles side was owned by his father, a white man, Fern couldn't stop looking at Big Ma. Big Ma knew Fern had something on her mind other than when she could lick the cake batter from the bowl.

"All right, Fern. What you want?"

"Big Ma," Fern said. "May I ask you a question?"

"You can ask," Big Ma said. "Don't mean I'll answer." Our grandmother knew a tough question when she heard it sneaking up.

"Big Ma, why you wear a wig and an Aunt Jemima rag?"

Big Ma wasn't expecting that one. Neither was I. "Aunt Jemima, *what*?" She stopped stirring. "Where's my belt?"

Instead of jumping behind me like I expected, Fern threw her head back and laughed, all teeth and her pink tongue showing. Then Big Ma laughed.

"Little rascal."

"But why, Big Ma? Why?"

I knew what Fern was asking. She wanted to know why Big Ma covered her hair when she had nothing to hide. Her hair wasn't too short or patchy and balding. She didn't have sores or bumps on her scalp. And even though she insisted we fry our hair to a crisp for Sunday services, she only had to pass the hot comb once, maybe twice, through her own hair on the one day of the week she deemed was proper to wear it without the wig. These days she took to cutting her hair in the back with her dress-pattern scissors to keep it from growing. I used to think it was because she liked wigs better than her own hair or that she thought black people's hair was bad hair. My mother felt differently about hair, which was one reason why she and Big Ma didn't get along. Cecile let her hair grow and grow in thick, natural braids, and she stuck pencils and pens in it.

I didn't understand Big Ma and her hair, but it would have never occurred to me to ask her about it, or ask why ours wasn't exactly like hers. But Fern was suddenly full of questions, starting with Big Ma's wigs, scarves, and hair.

"Fern Gaither," Big Ma said. "What do I look like I'm doing?"

"Stirring cake batter."

"That's right. Stirring. Now, suppose you took a big bite of lemon pound cake only to find more of your Big Ma's hair in it than lemon frosting?"

Fern knew when she was being outfoxed and wouldn't stand for it. "That's not what I mean, Big Ma. I want to know why you cover your own hair *all* the time. Except on Sundays. Then you only wear your Sunday hat with the feather."

"Because," Big Ma said, "no one needs to know my family business."

"You mean about your father's—"

"Never mind about my father's people and what's underneath this wig and scarf. Just you never mind! All you have to do is keep your hair clean, braided, and out of the cake batter." She went on stirring and muttering, and telling Fern to stop asking about things no one needs to know or there would be no cake for her.

Bambi's Mother

I could smell the smoke of something cooking while we were still in the woods making our way over to Miss Trotter's. I hoped no one noticed it until we were actually there, but Vonetta asked, "What's that?"

"Smells good!" Fern said—then quickly added, "And bad."

"Sure does," I agreed, pretending it was a mystery when I knew what was happening over at Miss Trotter's. I just didn't want Fern to start crying and pulling my arm for us to turn back to Ma Charles's house. We were here already and I didn't want to stay on our side of the creek. There was nothing to do at Big Ma's than watch the chickens fight over a cricket.

Miss Trotter and JimmyTrotter had a skinned deer roasting on a spit. JimmyTrotter cranked the handle to the spit and the deer turned around and around under a pit of burning coals. As we drew near, Fern, now close to me, close like she used to be, began to buckle at the knee. She was crying.

"Cut it out, baby," Vonetta said.

Fern wasn't up to fighting back. I could feel her folding into me.

"You cut it out," I told Vonetta. "She's your sister. Act like it."

Miss Trotter caught sight of us and waved. "Just in time for barbecue!" Both Miss Trotter and Ma Charles called any meat roasting in an outdoor fire "barbecue," when barbecue to us was sauce from the grocery store or sweet and spicy red dust on potato chips.

"No, no, no," Fern meowed into me. She tried to pull me backward. I pulled her forward. "Come on, Fern. You don't have to look at it. You can stay behind me." And of course Vonetta said, "Come on, baby." As much as I hated Vonetta's meanness, her taunting was enough to prop Fern up and move her feet forward just to show Vonetta she wasn't a baby. Fern grabbed a fistful of my top and stayed close to me.

The doneness of the animal going around and around said it had been cooking for a while. JimmyTrotter cut off pieces from the deer and put them in a pan and Miss

134

Trotter salted the pieces. She had already been eating the barbecue.

"Come on, girls," Miss Trotter said. "Come and get a treat."

Vonetta, eager to please, grabbed a piece of meat and bit into it. She chewed and yummed like the actress that she was.

Fern cried out, "That's no treat! That's Bambi's mother!"

JimmyTrotter started to tell his great-grandmother who Bambi was, but she put her hand up to him. "I know who Bambi's mother is. A make-believe deer in the pictures. You see, young'n, I know. Now get over here. Come on."

But Fern wouldn't move.

"You," my great-aunt said to me. "Let go of that girl." Although it was the other way around, Ferns fists wrapped around the bottom of my top, I loosened Fern's grip on my clothes and pushed her forward. "I don't bite children," she told Fern. "But I'll give 'em a taste of the hickory switch if they're bad." She meant to jolly Fern. Vonetta, who wasn't receiving any attention, rolled her eyes.

"Bambi is make-believe. This is a real deer. God-given to these woods to run about and breed."

"Aunt Miss Trotter, God doesn't want us to kill," Fern said. "We surely shall not!"

Fern said it the way Big Ma would have been proud of, although Big Ma wouldn't have appreciated that Fern talked back to Miss Trotter. Ma Charles, on the other hand, would have cackled and shaken her tambourine.

"God don't want us to kill each other, young'n," Miss Trotter said.

"Fern," my baby sister corrected. "God don't want us to kill each other, *Fern.*"

Miss Trotter turned to JimmyTrotter. "Boy, get me the biggest hickory switch you can find."

JimmyTrotter kept basting and salting the meat.

We ate the smoky venison meat except Fern, who ate a piece of bread. Miss Trotter waited for Fern to ask for more to eat but Fern never asked.

Miss Trotter said to Fern, "This animal made an offering to us all and you won't take it. Shame on you."

Fern shrugged.

"This animal gave us her meat. We'll share it with neighbors. And what we don't eat, we'll freeze for when there's nothing. She doesn't have much fat to her but she gave us her bones and hide. If it were a nice buck, I'd make good use of his horns. Everything the animal gives us is useful."

Fern thought long and hard like she was at her desk figuring out homework. It would have been nice if she'd said, "Yes, Aunt Miss Trotter."

Instead, she said, "Wish we could give it all back to her, Aunt Miss Trotter. Surely do."

* * *

That evening Miss Trotter filled a tin pan with sliced venison and wrapped it tightly, placing it in Vonetta's hands to carry. "Take this to your great-granny. She'd surely like to have it. But you don't have to tell her I shot it with Daddy's rifle. No. Don't tell her that. But if you need to tell her something, tell her I brought the doe down with one shot and cleaned out all the buckshot myself. That is, if she's worried about buckshot."

"I'll carry it," I said, reaching to take the pan from Vonetta.

"No, no," Miss Trotter said. "My dear one can carry it. She's strong and eats all of her food."

Her words were meant to make Fern feel badly, but Fern was in her world, humming and clapping. Almost the way Cecile did when she worked out her poems.

With the pan in her hands, Vonetta curtsied and we started back through the woods and over the creek. Vonetta's politeness lasted only until we were out of Miss Trotter's sight, and then she taunted Fern with the pan of cooked meat. I grabbed the pan out of Vonetta's hand with a swift yank. It was a good thing Miss Trotter had wrapped that pan well. I heard "I hate you, Delphine" all the way home, but I didn't care. Vonetta had to learn how to be a better sister to Fern, and I was going to teach her.

Vonetta pulled out all the stops and told Ma Charles almost word for word about how Miss Trotter shot the deer with her father's rifle and cleaned out the buckshot. I knew Miss Trotter threw in that bit about her father's rifle to rub salt in Ma Charles's heart. That Slim Jim Trotter left his rifle with Miss Trotter's mother and not hers. That it was probably true that Slim Jim Trotter spent more nights over the creek with Miss Trotter and her mother than here with Great-great-grandmother Livonia and Ma Charles when she was a little girl. But Slim Jim Trotter did make the chair Ma Charles sat in, and that was something.

If Miss Trotter had rubbed salt in Ma Charles's heart, our great-grandmother didn't let on. In fact, she clapped her hands and rubbed them together in anticipation when Big Ma unwrapped the meat.

"The Lord's working on Miss Trotter," Ma Charles said. "Let's eat."

When we sat down at the table, Fern said to Big Ma, "Why does Delphine get to say the dinner prayer? I can say it."

Uncle Darnell didn't have school that night and was seated at the table for supper. He winked at Fern.

Big Ma thought Bible school was "working on" Fern and that Fern had caught the spirit. Big Ma's face brightened and she said, "Bless your heart, Fern. Go on. Bless this table."

Fern cleared her throat, clasped her hands together, and lifted her turtle head high out of its shell.

Sorry, Chicken
Sorry, Deer
Sorry, Ham
Sorry, Cow
Sorry, Lamb
Chops are better
On a puppet
Or the lamb
They came from.
Baaaaaa—
But you can say
Amen.

Uncle Darnell said, "Amen," and snapped his fingers beatnik style, and I followed suit, adding a "Baaaaa" to my "Amen." Vonetta almost joined us but then stopped herself, refusing to take part in anything having to do with our uncle.

"The Lord's not pleased," Big Ma scolded. She pointed to Fern, who was proud of her protest poem disguised as our dinnertime prayer. "And you! Your head's swelling up—trying to act like your no-mothering mother—while the rest of you stays puny because you won't do right and eat what the Lord gave you. Mark my words. He won't let you grow if you can't offer Him a proper thanksgiving."

Ma Charles thought it was all hilarious. "Go on,

Rickets. That was a good prayer. Baaaaa."

Fern bowed her head low and grand over her plate of corn and string beans. "Afua," she proclaimed. "My poet name is Afua."

Short for Onchetty

"Look. Don't touch," JimmyTrotter warned. "You see this? See it?" He pointed to his airplane's red painted tail. "That was flown by the Ninety-ninth Pursuit Squadron all over Italy and North Africa."

We were in JimmyTrotter's room, pretending to love his model airplanes since there wasn't anything new to do or see. He talked on and on about the models his grandfather had given him, pointing out every little detail of his prized World War II fighter jet and the ugly army-green one, a bomber. The fighter jets were his. The bombers sat on Auggie's side of the room. Those, he wouldn't let us breathe on. Nor could we sit on Auggie's bed.

I, myself, was tired of war and anything to do with it.

Didn't they show enough war stuff on the news between the protests here and the shooting, bombing, and dying in Vietnam? We were lucky to get our uncle back from there and luckier to have him almost back to his old self, although Uncle D had long ago stopped telling us make-believe stories. I certainly wouldn't be keeping any model jeeps and choppers to remember the war going on, but JimmyTrotter thought his Red Tail war hawks and his brother's bomber jets were just grand. I was relieved when Miss Trotter called to us for a snack. We all came running.

Fern cheered when she saw that our snack was a slice of pie and warm milk and had nothing to do with animal meat. She sat right down and rubbed her hands together.

"Aunt Miss Trotter . . ." Fern began. Our great-aunt accepted that this is what Fern would call her. She raised her chin.

"Why don't you have a television?"

"Yeah, Great Miss Trotter." Vonetta threw in the "Great" to get a smile of approval. Ever since she stopped running back and forth between the sisters, delivering their poison pen stories, Vonetta had to work hard for Miss Trotter's attention. "Where's the TV?"

"Who says I don't have one?"

"They mean one that works, Great-grandma," Jimmy-Trotter said.

Miss Trotter swatted at JimmyTrotter's head but he leaned a quick left, like he knew it was coming, and she

142

missed. She and Ma Charles were so much alike I expected my great-aunt to turn to me and say, "Young'n, get me a switch."

"We have a television set," JimmyTrotter sang to Fern, all the while smiling at Miss Trotter. "It hasn't worked since George Wallace's inauguration."

Miss Trotter's face tightened and darkened. "Son, I told you about speaking that name in the house. Next time, go out to the manure pile and say it as free as you please."

JimmyTrotter laughed a good laugh, pie and milk in his open mouth. He collected himself and said, "Miss Trotter threw a pot at the TV just after the governor stood where Jefferson Davis had once stood, and shouted, 'Segregation now, segregation tomorrow, segregation forever.'"

"He said that out loud on television with the world watching?"

"Don't look so shocked, Brooklyn. You don't get more southern than Alabama."

Miss Trotter shook her head. "Hard to believe he didn't start out that way, but once he lost that first election he knew what he had to do, and old George's been doing it ever since. Some folks so evil, they'll sell their goodness to do bad."

"They just want power," I said.

"They don't care about the people," Vonetta added.

"Surely don't care about giving power to the people."

I enjoyed the sound of our voices following one another.

Sounded like a favorite song from the radio they no longer play, so when you hear it, you remember how things were.

JimmyTrotter's grin became devilish. "Y'all want to see the TV? That pot busted the screen something nice. We never got another one to replace it."

In spite of Miss Trotter's fussing and threatening to get a hickory switch, JimmyTrotter hopped up and went to the cabinet where the photograph of his great-great-grandparents rested. The yellowed doily that the framed photo sat upon draped slightly over the cabinet. The walnut cabinet made the television look like furniture that blended in with the living room set and reminded me of ours back in Brooklyn. That was, until Mrs. called the Salvation Army to haul it away. That was how we got our color TV and a plain television stand. No more wooden cabinet. That was also one of the biggest fights ever on Herkimer Street when Pa came home from work that evening.

JimmyTrotter opened the doors to the wooden cabinet with a fancy flourish so we could see what had been hidden inside. Our mouths were probably open and full of pie and milk when we saw it. The tube had been busted, all right, but like JimmyTrotter described it, there was something beautiful about it. I'd seen nothing like it. The surface seemed smooth and uncut, but the insides cracked in circles that went round and around.

"Charlotte was here!" Fern cried.

"Charlotte? I don't see any Charlotte," Vonetta said.

"The TV glass! It's round and cracked up like Charlotte's web." She skipped up to it and traced the glass.

"Ugh! You're such a believer in make-believe, baby."

"Stop it right now," I told one. "And don't touch that screen," I told the other. "Before you get cut."

Miss Trotter ambled up to the cabinet and traced her hand along the wood and even the glass, which was dusty. Then she picked up the framed photograph of Slim Jim Trotter with Ella Pearl, one of his two wives. She dusted the glass to the photograph, and said, "Afternoon, Papa. Mama," and set it back down on the television cabinet.

"My grandson got me that black-and-white set for Christmas." She said it full of pride, and then got a little sad. She was talking about JimmyTrotter's father, who I'd never met. For that matter, I'd never met JimmyTrotter's mother, his twin brother, or his grandmother, either.

JimmyTrotter said real fast, "If I want to see television, I go to Aunt Naomi's. She has a new set. Color *and* stereo."

"It's not brand-new. It's from Mr. Lucas," Vonetta said. "I think he likes Big Ma."

"What was your first clue, Sherlock?" I asked.

"Meanie," Vonetta said under her breath.

Miss Trotter told JimmyTrotter, "Go over the creek and stay if you like," although it was clear to me she didn't want him to go. "Just get the milking done, son. Poor

Sophie. Getting onchee with age."

"Onchee?" we all asked.

"Onchee. Short for onchetty." All the while Miss Trotter spoke, JimmyTrotter shook his head no behind her
back. He didn't have to. I knew a made-up word when I
heard one.

"That old gal prefers your touch to mine," Miss Trotter
said.

"You rush her, Miss Trotter." He said it both teasing
and respectful.

"I don't have all day to coax her to yield what she's supposed to yield in the first place. She's a milk cow. She's
supposed to milk."

"That's right, Great Miss Trotter," Vonetta said. "Lots of
us need milk in the morning."

"That's right, dear one," Aunt Miss Trotter cooed.

"She'd milk up a storm if her baby calf was here to
drink it," Fern said. "She surely would."

I took the plates and glasses from the table and left
them to fuss about milk and milking. JimmyTrotter followed me.

"Do you think it's a good idea to leave Miss Trotter alone?"

"I asked her if she wanted to come see the launch. I'd
even drive my father's car to bring her over—sheriff or no
sheriff." He rarely spoke about his father. And he never
spoke up against the sheriff.

"You can't convince her? Not even for the moon launch?"

He shrugged and laughed. "Thought you were catching on, cuz. It would take more than Apollo Eleven to get Miss Trotter to cross the creek."

"Try, cousin. At least try."

"Pretty please won't do it," he said. "Talk about onchee."

"She'll be all alone while we'll all be together." I stared him down but Jimmy stayed unchanged. "Onchee" ran on the Trotter side. I said, "If you won't do it, I will. I'll get Miss Trotter to come over to Ma Charles's."

"My great-granny likes being left to herself. But I'll pay money to see you get a woman who knows her mind to change it. Go on, Brooklyn. Let's see you do it."

"Fine." There was nothing better than a dare. I went marching up to Miss Trotter.

"Aunt Miss Trotter," I said. "Come with us and see the men land on the moon."

Aunt Miss Trotter chuckled. "Nothing wrong with my vision. I can see clear up to the moon from the porch. I can see all the comings and goings and shooting stars."

Good thing I didn't have a mouth full of pie. I laughed out loud at the thought of her being able to see what was happening on the moon.

She turned to Vonetta. "Young'n. Go out to the tree . . ." She didn't even finish her instructions. Vonetta was too happy to run out to the tree and scrap around among the twigs for a good licking stick. I heard her yell, "Ow!" Vonetta wanted me to get a taste so bad, she whacked herself with the twiggy candidates to get the one with the nastiest sting.

She galloped over to Miss Trotter with her switch. "Here, Miss Trotter. Get her."

"Don't you worry. I'm going to get her."

Unlike Vonetta, I knew my great-aunt was joking. She was so much like Ma Charles it hurt.

I coaxed and begged her to ride with JimmyTrotter in the station wagon and come over to see the men take off for the moon. I must have begged her ten different ways.

"Please, Miss Trotter."

"Please," Fern sang.

Vonetta only joined in because singing was involved and she had to make her voice louder than Fern's.

"Come with us tomorrow morning to watch the men land on the moon."

"There's nothing over there I need to see. No, sir!"

JimmyTrotter mouthed, "Told you so."

Miss Trotter chuckled and said, "What do you get if you poke a bear with a stick?"

Fern raised her paws and growled.

Vonetta said, "You get outta there fast!"

"Mark my words, young'ns. You poke a hole past this earth, you get something back."

"Like what?" I asked.

"Like that angry bear." She pointed to Fern and Fern growled on cue. "The earth doesn't take to being poked. Not its sky or beyond its sky. No, sir! The earth doesn't like it."

JimmyTrotter rolled his eyes.

Miss Trotter uttered a "Hmp." "Boy, I won't stop you from chasing your heart's desire. No, no. I won't deprive you of things that fly. It comes to you naturally." She said to me, "But I won't go marching across that creek to her mother's house." I was sure she meant our great-great-grandmother Livonia's house. "She'll have to walk to me. I won't walk to her."

"But why, Miss Trotter? We'll all be there," I said. "All of us, together."

"Yes. All of you. All her generations. Daughter, grandson, great-grands." She shook her head willfully. "I won't go so she can talk to me as if I'm a beggar looking at her generations, when she knows I hunger for my own. No. I won't go sit in her mother's house."

Talk about onchetty. Those were her final words.

When we left, she said like always, "Go on and goodbye, if you call that gone."

Jimmy Trotter said, "Pay up, Brooklyn."

As soon as we got home, I said to Ma Charles, just to see her reaction, "We asked Miss Trotter to come and watch the astronauts take off for the moon."

Ma Charles perked up like I knew she would, which told me I had to try harder to get Miss Trotter to cross over the creek or go around on the road.

"Coming here? My sister?" She turned to Uncle Darnell and said, "Kill a chicken," and to me she said, "And you pluck it and clean it. I know you know how." To Big Ma she said, "I want her to be stuffed till she can't walk, so start on a cobbler and drown it in sugar. Daughter, drown it good. I won't let hers be the last hospitality offered, showing off with her barbecue venison. It's a shame we don't have a hog to kill and butcher. A crime and a shame."

"Hooray for Wilbur!" Fern cried. But no one paid her any mind.

But now, seeing my great-grandmother excited, I felt bad and said, "She's not coming."

Then Ma Charles felt bad about getting excited. "It makes me no never mind if she stays on her side of the creek."

Big Ma started to fan herself. "See what you done?" she scolded me.

"Yeah," Vonetta said. "See, meanie?"

"See what?" Fern asked.

Big Ma wagged her finger at me. "You can't get my mother's heart to racing. She's an old woman."

Ma Charles rocked herself like a child on a hobby horse, wearing the mile-long pout I was used to seeing on my sisters. "I knew she wasn't coming," she said. "I knew it."

Like a Bird in the Sky

"I don't care what you say. Man has gone too far." Big Ma whomped her black Bible against the arm of her easy chair and pulled herself up from its comfy cushions. "He should know his place."

"Amen, daughter!" Ma Charles raised her tambourine and gave it a good shake.

"Forgive man his arrogance, Lord God."

"Forgive, Lord."

"Man pushes his arrogant self out, poking holes through the sky; God will sling His arrows back down on man through those holes in a mighty rain."

"Send your arrows, smite him down, Lord."

"But the Lord is merciful. Oh yes! He can surely grant man a mercy."

"A mercy, daughter!" Ma Charles shouted, happy that church was going on in her living room on Wednesday morning. "A mercy."

"A spacecraft is a man-made thing."

"Speak, daughter."

"It may go far, but it cannot reach heaven."

The tambourine shook and its metal disks rang out.

"It cannot reach the Lord though it will trespass on his holy place!"

Tambourine!

Big Ma and Ma Charles asked all to repenteth: the astronauts, mission control in Houston for thinking they had control, and the TV station for cutting off the morning gospel hour to broadcast the space launch. And yet we all gathered in Ma Charles's living room while I angled for a better picture of the crowds gathered outside the launch pad down in Florida. Pastor Curtis, who had on Sunday proclaimed the Apollo mission an ungodly endeavor, said he'd be taking Wednesday morning prayer service off so he wouldn't miss the liftoff. Even golden-framed Jesus's eyes were on the launch.

"To the right. Yeah, Cousin Del. Now angle it toward the window. Yeah. Keep angling."

JimmyTrotter wouldn't let us nickname him, but he called me "cuz," "Del," and "Brooklyn" every chance he got. I pulled out the left antenna rod as far as it could go and aimed it from one corner of the window to the other.

I pointed the metal rod and froze as JimmyTrotter, my sisters, Uncle D, and Mr. Lucas hollered out, "Hot," "Hotter," "To the right," "More," "A little left," and then "Aww!" Watching television in Autauga County, Alabama, wasn't like watching TV in our house on Herkimer Street. At home in Brooklyn, you turned the dial six or seven times to see what was on the other channels. Then you fixed the antenna when you settled on a show. Down in this part of Alabama, one turn to the left and one turn back to the right were our only choices. And if there was an electrical storm, there was no television to watch, period. No radio. No lights. No nothing. During electrical storms Big Ma and Ma Charles allowed only the dark, a candle, and prayer, although my sisters and I played Old Maid and Go Fish.

Finally, a glimpse of the giant rocket, JimmyTrotter's precious Saturn V, materialized out of snow, fuzz, and horizontal lines. We all cheered. The second I stepped away the picture snowed up and the sound crackled.

"I'm not standing here holding this antenna," I said.

Vonetta seized her opportunity. "I will!" I stood aside and let Vonetta do what she did naturally: cause all attention to be pulled her way. She raised the antenna rods together to start over and arranged the rods in a leaning V.

"That's it! Bravo, cuz!" JimmyTrotter shouted to Vonetta. "We have a perfect picture!"

Vonetta froze, then backed away from the antenna, carefully and dramatically, her arms outstretched in the leaning V shape of the left and right antennae until she sat down. I hated to admit it, but it worked. Furthermore, the picture stayed sharp.

"See, Delphine? I can do things better than you." She stuck her tongue out and I socked her in the arm. Not hard. Just enough to let her know I was still older.

"Cut it out," JimmyTrotter said firmly, like he was Pa or something. I rolled my eyes and Vonetta grinned. I'd get her later. JimmyTrotter considered the matter settled. He turned to Uncle Darnell. "Cousin, did you fly in any planes in the army?"

"Don't ask him any of that war business," Big Ma said. "That's over and done with."

"Yeah," Vonetta said, "because he just might—"

"Shut up, Vonetta."

"Now both of you, stop it," Uncle Darnell said. "Y'hear?" Now *that* was Pa's voice. Sharp and short. When we piped down he smiled at JimmyTrotter as if he hadn't raised his voice at all. "I rode in 'em. Got evac'd by helo."

Jimmy thought that was cool although it sounded like spy code to me.

"We flew in a big silver plane," Fern said. "The ride was too bumpy."

JimmyTrotter patted her head until she wriggled away. "I don't want to be a passenger in a plane," he said. "I want

154

to fly them. I'm saving for lessons."

"With Old Man Crump?" Mr. Lucas asked. He almost coughed.

"Yes, sir," Jimmy Trotter said. I mimicked, "Yes, sir," just hating the South in him. I didn't care if he caught me or not.

Both Mr. Lucas and Uncle Darnell shared a laugh about Old Man Crump. "Son," Mr. Lucas said, "I know some World War Two cats who can show you a thing or two if you really want to fly. Leave Crump and his crop duster alone."

"You know that's right," Uncle Darnell said.

"I wouldn't mind getting into an aviation program," JimmyTrotter said. "I just want to fly."

Fern piped, "Like a bird in the sky."

Ma Charles laughed. "Scratch your back for feathers, son. Can't feel a one? I guess God told you." There was a twinkle in her eyes so I knew she meant him no harm. Of course not. She just loved JimmyTrotter.

"Oh, son," Big Ma said. "They don't let coloreds fly planes." Uncle D said, *"Ma,"* but Big Ma wouldn't stop. "And I don't blame them. Say what you want, but a colored man's mind isn't made for flying an airplane. Too many dials and levers. Too many decisions to make. The colored man can be a good many things. A preacher. An insurance salesman. A mayor of a colored town. Educated, respectable things, but he can't go thinking he can do everything and anything. He can't go above himself. Suppose he makes a mistake up in the air with all the people watching?"

Mr. Lucas said in a low, sad voice, "Ophelia . . ." but JimmyTrotter said nothing. *Nothing.* And if I weren't a little steamed at him for always taking Vonetta's side I would have said black people have the power to be whatever they wanted. I would have said don't let the Man keep you down, even though this time the Man was my grandmother. But JimmyTrotter was happy to be oppressed and that was fine with me.

Uncle D, Mr. Lucas, JimmyTrotter, Ma Charles, Big Ma, Fern, and I all looked toward the TV screen. Our excitement grew as the picture and sound came in clearer and clearer. The camera switched from the Saturn V rocket in Florida to mission control in Houston, a roomful of men in mostly white short-sleeve shirts, and then to the crowd, where our former president and his wife, LBJ and Lady Bird Johnson, stood squinting, smiling, and looking up. We cheered when we saw a black person in the crowd. At last!

Clouds of white smoke seemed to float out of the tall rocket, held up by the hugging arms of a kind of straight Eiffel Tower. JimmyTrotter said the white clouds were there to keep the rocket cool, but I doubted anything could keep that rocket cool.

Every ten or fifteen seconds or so, the mission control

person counted down by "T-minus" and threw in "We are a go," while clouds of smoke billowed and they showed the rocket from close up and then from far away.

The countdown clock showing on the screen was now closing in on two minutes and counting. I doubted they could stop the launch if they wanted to. The Saturn V rocket seemed too monstrous to be made to heel by the control room in Houston.

I hoped my parents were also tuned in to the launch and counting along with us—Pa and Mrs. by TV and Cecile by radio. I knew my father and stepmother would be thoroughly amazed, and my mother would see the act of man landing on the moon as cause to write an oppressed woman's poem. There was nothing Cecile couldn't turn into a poem. Even so, it was nice to picture all of us watching or listening to the same thing at the same time. But if Miss Trotter showed up on Ma Charles's porch, now that would be something to see.

Everyone was exited but Fern, who folded her arms. "Is this it? Is this the blastoff?"

I knew that "Phooey" look on Fern's face. She probably felt gypped about the event that the news kept promising would be the most exciting thing for mankind to ever witness. As far as she could see, there wasn't any magic. Just a roomful of men sitting at control panels, crowds of people waiting for something to happen, and a tall space rocket with a lot of white smoke surrounding it.

"Hang on," JimmyTrotter told Fern. "It's coming. Just don't blink."

Fern moved away from JimmyTrotter and sat closer to me. Vonetta mouthed, *Baby*, and Fern kicked her. I moved Fern to my left side to keep them separated. At least someone kicked Vonetta. That was good enough for me.

The mission control man reported that one of the astronauts said, "It feels good," although I doubted sitting on a million tons of rocket fuel could feel good at all. JimmyTrotter's precious Saturn V rocket stood ready and Ma Charles shook her tambourine. Before we knew it, the Eiffel Tower's arms were letting go of the rocket and we were all counting down with mission control. Even Big Ma and Ma Charles. All of us.

Five

Four

Three

Two . . .

Klan

The next day JimmyTrotter told Miss Trotter he was hopping over the creek to watch more of Apollo 11. "I'll be back in the morning for milking. I'm gone."

"I'm gone!" Vonetta and Fern mocked.

"Go on, then," Miss Trotter called after them. "If you call that gone."

Vonetta wanted to ride JimmyTrotter's bike, and he said, "It's yours while you're here. Ride it all you want."

"Hear that?" Vonetta said to me.

"Just don't go too far ahead of us," I told her. "Hear that? And walk it over the bridge, Vonetta. Walk it!"

Vonetta sucked her teeth and ran off to get the bike. She'd better run.

JimmyTrotter smiled. He thought it was funny, the way Vonetta and I fussed with each other. But then, he was used to it, seeing how Miss Trotter and Ma Charles kept up their sniping from the Trotter side of the creek to the Charles side.

Ma Charles was delighted to have JimmyTrotter in the house, whether he was dropping off milk bottles or bringing one of Miss Trotter's remedies that Ma Charles had no intention of trying. I could see the personal victory swell up in her whenever she had her sister's great-grandson under her roof, at her table, or in front of her television.

"Make sure you feed him well, daughter," she said to Big Ma. "Send him back over the creek with some meat on his bones." She shook her head in make-believe sorrow. "Poor Miss Trotter. So fragile she can't lift a pot."

JimmyTrotter laughed and said, "Great-granny feeds me just fine."

"Now that's how you're supposed to raise them! Loyal and respectful," Ma Charles said. "That's right, boy. Don't tell on your old great-granny."

JimmyTrotter gave her a "Yes, ma'am."

Big Ma set a plate before JimmyTrotter with the same amount she'd heap onto Pa's or Uncle Darnell's plates.

"Why can't I get that much?" I asked.

"I'm trying to grow you into a young lady. Not a horse."

To that, Fern neighed and Vonetta whinnied and shot in a "Greedy gut." Vonetta felt safe at the table, seated out

160

of kicking range, next to her protector, JimmyTrotter.

"Throw another chop on her plate, daughter," Ma Charles said. "And some butter beans. Some gravy. Can't have her running across the creek eating up all your great-granny's weeds and berries," she told JimmyTrotter. "Go on, daughter. A nice big piece. We're doing mighty fine on this side of the creek. Make sure you tell your old granny how well you're fed."

"The Lord don't like ugly," Big Ma told her mother.

"Any more'n he likes you celebrating the troubles of others, be they rich or poor."

Big Ma had taken to reading her supermarket gossip news out in the open, and Ma Charles was none too pleased about "these chirrens today." The constant coverage of the space program had taken its toll on Big Ma, and she missed hearing about other news in the world.

"Don't know why you care so much about the troubles of rich folk," Ma Charles scolded. "Daughter, I might not agree with men poking up in God's heaven, but that's news. Now, if you had a husband—"

"Come on, son, and watch your 'Pollo 'Leven," Big Ma said, knocking off vowels like she was knocking off the suggestion that she needed to get married. "May God show them astronauts and their families a mercy."

JimmyTrotter scooted before the television and I scooted along with him. I wasn't into the space race, but there was no way I'd miss the moon landing.

* * *

161

I almost fell asleep on JimmyTrotter's shoulder but Caleb bayed long, fitful notes and wouldn't stop. We all looked around. A rumbling pounded beneath me. JimmyTrotter sprang up in one motion and ran to the window. Caleb bayed on and on.

Big Ma said, "Boy! Get from that window! You know better."

"I want to see them, Aunt Ophelia."

"You'll see nothing. You know what it is."

"See what?" I wanted to know.

"Klan riding," JimmyTrotter said. "Sounds like a dozen of 'em."

"Riding horses?" Fern was excited.

"Get from that window," Ma Charles said to Fern. "It's no Wild West show."

"I want to see the horses," Fern said.

"And I told you"—Big Ma was firm—"there's no horses to see."

Before I had sense enough to stop myself, I was in the window—not even crouching, but every inch of me standing tall. The riders had long ridden past us and into the pines. It was too dark to see horses but I could still feel their hooves punching the ground our house stood on. I could see white ghosts moving in the night, and torches against the black. I could see the sheets. White sheets.

"Get out that window, gal! Get out!" Big Ma shouted at my back.

I might as well have been twenty-one and not twelve. In my bones I knew I had outgrown my fear of Big Ma and that there was nothing she could do to me, but I stepped away from the window. I was both afraid of the Klan and fascinated by them. They weren't in a newspaper article or on the evening news; they were here. I felt them pounding their horses' hooves into our land, and saw them riding past the fields and into the pines. The way Caleb sang, loud and sad, I couldn't tell if he was baying at them or if he wanted to be with them. It was a long, sad song.

"JimmyTrotter." Ma Charles's voice had lost its cackling. "Don't worry about your great-granny. None of this is new to her. She knows what to do. She'll be all right."

"Yes'm."

There was no sympathy for me. Big Ma scolded, "Delphine. I can't understand why you went running to that window, looking for trouble. I don't care what kind of power they're shouting about in Oakland and in Brooklyn. You don't know nothing about nothing down here."

"Besides," Ma Charles said, "no secret who's underneath them hoods and sheets."

"Ma," Big Ma steamed, "I'm trying to tell her something to save her life while she's down here."

Ma Charles behaved as if she didn't hear and that in itself was funny, but I didn't dare crack a smile. "Just count all those who have horses in this one-cow town."

She said "hoss" with no *r*.

Fern said, "Two-cow town," but no one was listening.

"There's a way to stay alive and a way to be dead," Big Ma said. "Your father surely didn't send you down here to be among the dead. He surely didn't." Fern mimicked her. *He surely didn't.* "That's one phone call I don't intend to make to your Pa: to inform him his child is among the dead, strung up or shot up by the KKK. Girl, don't give me cause to make that call."

Ma Charles shook her head and said, "Poor Caleb. Only reason that dog carried on is he sniffed out his litter kin when the Klan rode by. He was just barking and pining for his brother and sisters. That's all."

JimmyTrotter nodded in agreement. "It's been years but Caleb most likely smells them whenever the sheriff drives by."

It took a few seconds for me to hear what Ma Charles and JimmyTrotter were saying. Saying as calm as they might say Mr. Lucas grows pecan trees.

"The sheriff's the Klan?" I asked. My voice loud, excited. No wonder cousin JimmyTrotter had given him a bunch of "Yes, sir"s.

Ma Charles nodded. "All the Charleses on the white side are Klan. Then there's my Henry's people." She beamed. "The colored side."

"Ma!" Big Ma said. "Yawl stop talking about this. No one needs to know this stuff."

It was all still swimming in my head faster than I could really grab hold of it, let alone accept it. "Our relatives are KKK?"

"That's not your relative," Big Ma said. "Just let it lie."

Ma Charles said, "If the bloodhound don't let it lie, why should she? That's not a lazy dog. That's a sad dog. Miss his kin. Calling out for all them pups he nipped at." Then she said thoughtfully, "Maybe I'll call Davey Lee. See if there's a female for Caleb."

"You mean have the Klan come over to this house?" My head was spinning. My heart was beating fast. This was crazy. Alabama crazy.

Ma Charles did me the way she did Big Ma. She went on like she didn't hear how crazy it all sounded.

"That poor dog needs a wife like you need a husband."

"A mercy, Lord. Throw me down a mercy, please, Lord. She's going to wake up every Trotter, Charles, and Gaither with this old stuff."

Keeping Up
with the Kennedys

On the second day after the space launch Big Ma said to JimmyTrotter, "Now, son, you've watched enough flying spaceships for today. I need to see my program."

By "her program" she meant the other channel, whose midday news show was more interested in the drowning of that secretary in Cape Cod than in the moon mission. The astronauts could have shaken hands with moon men on live television. As long as one of the Kennedys was in the news, Big Ma had to know all about it.

JimmyTrotter was too respectful to utter an "Aw, shucks" and too old to poke out his bottom lip and pout. He scooted up like he had been sitting on hot coals and said, "Yes'm, Aunt Ophelia." *Yes'm*, and not the full-out "ma'am," a word that belonged back in the slavery days.

He strode over and bent low to kiss Ma Charles. "I have to be going. See about Miss Trotter."

"You stay put, son," Ma Charles fussed. "You can see your spacemen right here." But at this point, they weren't showing the telecast of the real Apollo 11 spacecraft, only a simulation of it racing toward the moon. And at times we heard the astronauts' voices going "Roger this" and "Roger that" to mission control.

JimmyTrotter grabbed his basket of eggs and went back over to kiss Big Ma, who wiped his kiss away like she'd been buzzed by a fly. He waved to me a good-bye and left.

"See that, daughter?" Ma Charles said. "Don't you feel ashamed, chasing that boy outta here? Heaven knows what he'll tell his old great-granny about our un-Christianly kindness."

Big Ma said, "Mama, I can't listen to this program and listen to you." That was practically a "Hush up," although our grandmother didn't dare say those words to her mother.

Ma Charles went on tsk-tsking about "these chirren today."

"I'll tell you, daughter. I won't be here forever to take care of you."

Big Ma uttered a faint "Yes, Ma," mesmerized by the darkness and glow of black-and-white photos of the sorry

Ted Kennedy and the drowned blond secretary who could not be saved. I doubted my grandmother blinked once during the news show—even when there was no more actual news to report about the drowning. Her eyes were pulled into the television screen like JimmyTrotter's had been as he hoped for a glimpse of the astronauts instead of those simulations and the broadcasts of mission control. Like JimmyTrotter, Big Ma was hoping for more.

I knew which parts Big Ma liked. She liked the parts about how the Kennedys were like kings and queens in America and how tragedy followed anyone named Kennedy. Big Ma wouldn't vote for a Kennedy, but in secret, she liked both the ballroom gowns and the pillbox hats Jackie wore as Mrs. Kennedy, and frowned upon the slacks and shades she wore as Mrs. Onassis. She liked seeing the young, important Kennedy families, and in her way, she liked the sadness of the country weeping for them. It was the story of them that she liked. When the newscaster gravely reminded us that this new tragedy sealed the final ending to "our nation's Camelot story," Big Ma said, "Yes, sir. It surely does."

Ma Charles wasn't finished fussing with Big Ma. "But you'll send me to my rest worrying about my only child."

Big Ma said, "Don't worry on my account. The Lord will provide for me."

"Wish you took as much interest in a husband like you do in them Kennedys."

"Can't hear, Ma."

"Won't hear," her mother corrected. "You know, Elijah Lucas won't be eligible forever. One day you'll look over and—"

Big Ma finished it for her: "Smell his wife's pecan pies cooling on the windowsill." Big Ma added, "I have a husband waiting for me in heaven. Don't need another." She pulled herself out of the chair to turn up the volume on the television and then plopped back down.

"Can I make you some tea?" I asked my great-grandmother, who continued her tsk-tsking even if Big Ma couldn't be moved.

"All I've done, I've done for that one there." Ma Charles pointed at her daughter, but Big Ma refused to look her way.

"I'll boil the water," I said.

"I don't want tea," Ma Charles snapped. "Tea won't fix this curse."

"What curse?"

Big Ma sighed, long and heavy, a moan beneath it. Still, her eyes stayed pulled toward the newscaster.

Ma Charles began to tell me about the curse. That Big Ma had to wait ten years before she had Junior, my pa. And then another dozen years before Darnell came.

"Maybe she was sick," I offered quietly. I thought about Mrs. at home sick, throwing up at the sight and smell of food.

"Sick? What sick? I tell you, it was a curse put on my own child to get back at me." My nose and mouth scrunched up in disbelief but Ma Charles went on. "Nothing would give my father's other daughter more pleasure than to see my generations cut off before they got started. The Lord shows you, be careful what you wish on others. You'll wish it on yourself." She almost smiled, but then fixed her face, probably so as not to gloat over Miss Trotter's family tragedy.

The SpideR Has LaNded

The lunar module separated from the command module and landed on the moon's surface that Saturday afternoon. We saw a simulation of the landing but we heard the real thing. The minute the lunar module touched the moon's floor, all of us watching TVs and listening to the broadcast became earthlings, waiting for the two astronauts in the lunar module to step outside and onto the moon. I had a time getting Vonetta and Fern to stay inside to watch the landing, let alone wait for the two astronauts to climb out and walk on the moon. Vonetta and Fern had been good earlier, watching and listening as the space shuttle orbited around the moon, taking its time to fire off another rocket to land. When the spacecraft finally separated into two ships, one landing and the other one staying up in space, we all cheered. Big Ma and Ma Charles prayed. But that seemed to be all there was to it. The spacecraft sat on the moon for hours and Vonetta and Fern wanted to go outside and run around with the chickens before the sun went down.

"Call us when Martians come."

"Martians are on Mars."

"Call us when the Moonies come."

"There's no such thing as Moonies."

"If there's Martians, there's Moonies."

"Just call us when something happens."

Off they ran.

The only thing happening was a lot of radioing between mission control and the astronauts. JimmyTrotter took a chance and ran through the pines and over the creek to check on Butter and to get whatever afternoon milk Sophie was willing to give. He came back by six for supper, which Ma Charles was only too glad to have Big Ma heap on his plate. We told him he'd missed the little silver men that came to greet the lunar module, but he pulled out his transistor radio and laughed in our faces.

It was long after our bedtime and still nothing had happened. I didn't have to ask. Ma Charles told Big Ma, "Let 'em see it," and Big Ma fussed and went to bed. We cheered our little victory, but Vonetta and Fern had drifted off on our mountain of pillows and sheets spread out on the floor.

I glanced at my Timex. If the astronauts planned to climb out of the Eagle, they had to do it soon, or the only thing we'd be seeing at midnight would be the picture on the TV screen of the American flag or the Indian chief posted at the end of the broadcast day. I wanted my sisters to see the astronauts on the moon almost as badly as I had wanted them to see the Jackson Five on TV for the first time. I knew they shouldn't miss any moon walking but I found myself, like Mr. Lucas and Ma Charles, drifting off to sleep.

Around ten forty-five that night, JimmyTrotter poked me in the shoulder. "Cousin Del, it's about to happen."

"You sure?"

"Any minute." Even Walter Cronkite's voice had that quiet excitement of a sportscaster announcing a big-deal golf putt. It was about to happen.

JimmyTrotter tugged on Mr. Lucas's sleeve and Mr. Lucas pretended he'd been awake. He gently nudged Ma Charles and then called out, "Ophelia. Come on out. Ophelia, come on before you miss it." Big Ma took to hiding in her room when Mr. Lucas stayed to watch the moon mission.

Even Big Ma wanted to witness the astronauts walking on the moon. She joined us in the living room, but wouldn't sit in the empty chair next to Mr. Lucas.

I tried to get Fern up while Jimmy pulled Vonetta's ear. Not hard, but playful. Light. I'd never thought of anyone besides our parents, Fern, and once, Uncle D, really and truly liking Vonetta. JimmyTrotter not only liked Vonetta, he adored her. She woke up smiling at him.

Fern stretched and opened her eyes. She saw the simulated spacecraft and sleepily sang, "The itsy-bitsy spider dropped on the yellow moon." Even on the color television screen, the moon wasn't yellow or silver. It was whitish gray. And dull. But Fern did get the spider part right. The lunar module looked more like a four-legged spider than an eagle. But I'm sure it wouldn't have been the same if the astronaut had said "The Spider has landed" when they first touched down on the moon's surface.

Finally, we were watching the real thing. The real-live broadcast and not a simulation with actors playing the parts of the astronauts. Finally, the words "Live from the surface of the moon" showed up fuzzy but readable on the television screen, and we were seeing the real moon. We all cheered. Big Ma said, "May God have mercy," and Ma Charles shook her tambourine. The snowy figure of an astronaut in a padded white suit with a bubble helmet and backpack climbed down the ladder of the Eagle in what seemed like slow motion and did what I never thought I'd see. He stepped foot on the moon. The words "Man on Moon" flashed before our excited and astonished eyes.

Big Ma gasped. From the corner of my eye I saw a

motion from Mr. Lucas to Big Ma. He reached over to touch her hand. I didn't look on but I noticed my grandmother hadn't snatched her hand from Mr. Lucas the way she wiped away kisses and shooed off hugs.

The television console speakers crackled. JimmyTrotter lifted up his hands and asked everyone to be quiet so we could hear Walter Cronkite and the astronauts. Cronkite said, "Armstrong is on the moon. Neil Armstrong—thirty-eight-year-old American—standing on the moon!"

JimmyTrotter shouted, "We won the space race!"

It wasn't long before gunshots went off in the air from miles away.

Two things sprang to mind as I watched one astronaut on the moon, and then another astronaut running, hopping, and frolicking on the moon. That there was a third astronaut hovering above in the command module far above the hubbub. While the two below tested their weightlessness, picked up samples of whatever moonie-eyed lovers looked up to, and marked up the moon's surface with moon boot tracks, the third astronaut was left behind holding everything together.

The other thing that sprang to mind was that the moon was beautiful at night from a distance, but it surely was a lonely place up close.

Got Milk?

Once the two astronauts had walked on the moon the excitement seemed to die down for everyone except JimmyTrotter, who listened to updates on his pocket radio and watched Apollo 11 news on our television set when Big Ma's programs weren't on.

Soon everything would go back to normal. The astronauts would return to Earth to their families and we'd forget we were all earthlings. I thought it was funny when one of the astronauts called their space capsule a "happy home." If that tight little spaceship was a happy home, then that astronaut's real home must have been a sad one.

A happy home had nothing to do with three men in a bubble eating sawdust food and watching pencils floating in the air. A happy home meant having everyone under one roof, sitting around the table, eating a peach cobbler or pecan pie.

I thought about Pa and Mrs. Then I thought about the baby. Having a little brother wouldn't be so bad. Or maybe another sister.

Uncle Darnell came in that morning from having worked an all-night shift. He gave Big Ma the local newspaper with her gossip paper folded within it and Big Ma went back to her room and left the television to JimmyTrotter.

Vonetta, who wasn't speaking to Uncle Darnell, poked Fern.

Fern poked her back, but asked, "Uncle D, did you buy a quart of milk?"

"Depends," he said. "Who's asking?"

Vonetta gasped, her eyebrows raised high. "You got it?"

"Got what?" he asked. If ever I missed my uncle's dimples, it was now that he didn't smile at this perfect opportunity to tease his favorite niece and let his dimples show.

"Milk," she answered.

"Did you ask me to bring home a quart of milk?" No dimples.

She was silent.

Ma Charles stood up, her finger pointed. "No milk but cow's milk straight from the cow! Not in this house."

177

I spoke up. "But Ma Charles, store milk comes from cows. At the dairy farm."

"I know what I said and why. They don't have grass at the dairy factory," Ma Charles said. "And if they do, believe me, those factory cows don't graze on grass that springs out of dirt. I'm not ignorant," she said. "I've seen 'em penned and chained worse than convicted killers. No, sir," she declared. "You won't pour a bowl of prison milk in this house." As ludicrous as she sounded, she meant it.

"I'll stop at the McDaniels' farm this evening. Bring home some milk," Uncle D said.

"Shouldn't have to drive six miles out of the way when we got fresh milk over the creek," Ma Charles said.

"Auntie, I can't help that Sophie's drying up before Butter's ready," JimmyTrotter said.

"Course you can't," she said. "It's that great-granny of yours that put something on that cow to keep her from milking. She'd kill a calf to see that my great-grands stay deprived of milk, and no one needs milk more than Rickets here. Bones just as weak and puny."

Jimmy smiled a little, the way Pa looks away and smiles when Big Ma says something crazy, and there was no shortage of craziness down here in Alabama. "Auntie . . ."

"Oh, I know she does it to spite me. She sees all my kin are here. It's nothing but pure spite and you can tell her I said so."

I opened my mouth to say whatever Big Ma would

have said if she wasn't squirreled away reading her gossip paper, but JimmyTrotter gave me a head shake. Like, *No. Let her go on.*

"I know how that sister of mine is. You tell her, I know about the curse."

Only Ma Charles and Miss Trotter could get themselves riled over things that made sense only to them. There was such a thing as being too much alike and equally stubborn.

"As long as I have milk for my cornflakes," Vonetta said, "I don't care about anything else."

Pure T Spite

Maybe spite was catching. Uncle Darnell had left for school and returned without the milk he had promised. Furthermore, regardless of what Ma Charles had said, JimmyTrotter came over the next morning with far less than the two quarts of milk that he normally brought.

"I don't know what I'm going to do about Sophie," JimmyTrotter said, probably hoping Ma Charles would take pity. "I might have to take her to town for beef."

I prayed Fern didn't catch on and that Vonetta wasn't mean enough to explain what JimmyTrotter said about taking Sophie to town.

"You tell your old great-granny: no milk, no eggs," Ma Charles said. "An understanding is an understanding."

"Auntie, I brought all that Sophie gave."

"And it don't fill a bottle," Ma Charles said.

"It's just enough for one bowl of cereal, and I called it," Vonetta said.

"I refuse to take the insult," Ma Charles said. "Take those three drops of milk on back to her."

"I want it!" Vonetta wailed.

"You'll take nothing," Ma Charles said.

JimmyTrotter said, "I don't know about Sophie. I expected at least another two months from her."

"It's because they sold her boy calf to the butcher. For hamburgers," Vonetta said to Fern. I could have smacked Vonetta. Smacked the smile off her face.

"Vonetta!"

"Stop treating her like a baby," Vonetta snapped back. She had no idea of how close I came to popping her. "You love to baby your baby." To Fern she said, "And you stop acting like a baby. Pa and Mrs. can't diaper you *and* the new baby."

I reached out to snag Vonetta but she was quick and leaped away, laughing.

"Don't let me catch you," I told her.

"Stop picking on Vonetta," JimmyTrotter said.

Fern began to cry for Sophie's calf. I held out my arms and she stepped into them. I sniffed the top of her head, which was sweet from coconut oil and tangled from no combing. I rocked her as she cried.

Vonetta rolled her eyes and mouthed, *Baby*. Big Ma used to say there wasn't a human being as unfeeling and selfish as Cecile. I could say the same thing about Vonetta.

JimmyTrotter pleaded to let him have a few more eggs but Ma Charles sat up straight in the pine chair her father made, looking every bit as "onchee" as her sister. "She's doing this to pay me back because all my folks are living and all hers—but one—have gone to glory. I never heard of anything more spiteful."

"Auntie," JimmyTrotter said, "Miss Trotter wouldn't do anything to keep Sophie from milking. That's just—" He was too respectful to call an elder crazy but it was Alabama crazy. "She wouldn't do anything like that."

"Heaven knows what she dropped in the grass. Plenty of weeds around to kill a cow or dry her up," Ma Charles said. "Pure T spiteful."

"Auntie, you know that's not true. We depend on Sophie and Butter too," he said. "There's no cowbane for miles. I always check where they graze."

Big Ma had heard all the spite and evil going on and emerged from her room. "Mama," she scolded, "the Lord don't like meanness." Then she said to JimmyTrotter, "Son, you take as many eggs as you need."

Ma Charles shook the milk bottle. "That's two eggs and no more."

"Delphine," Big Ma said. "Go in the coop and get a dozen eggs."

"A dozen?" Ma Charles said. "A dozen?"

For once, JimmyTrotter didn't want to be around for the fussing between his aunts. "I know where everything is." He got up and was out the back door before it would start.

"Should be ashamed of yourself," Big Ma scolded. "You're no better than these children."

"It's you who should be ashamed," Ma Charles said. "Setting the wrong example for your grands. Showing them they don't have to live up to their word. Being disrespectful to your own mother. Raising my pressure."

"Let's help JimmyTrotter," I told Fern, although he didn't need our help. I didn't much care what Vonetta did but she trailed behind us. JimmyTrotter had already taken what he needed and was crossing the field, heading into the pines.

He'd left enough eggs for us to gather and bring inside.

"I want my milk for my cornflakes. It's all that stupid cow's fault." Vonetta pouted.

"Don't call her that," Fern said. "She's not stupid. She's sad. She wants her baby cow and her baby cow is gone for good."

"If you call dead gone," Vonetta cackled in Miss Trotter's voice.

"Vonetta!"

She stood there with cow eyes.

I didn't have to beat Vonetta. I knew exactly how to get

her. I planted one hand on my hip and pointed with the other. "That's why you don't have *real* friends. Just some-time-y, fake friends who take your things. But you're too chickenhearted to stand up to your fake friends so you jump on your little sister every chance you get. And your sometime-y, fake friends must laugh at you behind your back and in front of your face because they know you're too chicken to do anything about it. Serves you right. You're selfish, a show-off, whiny—"

"And mean to your little sister!"

"That especially," I said.

Vonetta seemed to bask in our insults, wearing each one proudly. "I don't care what you call me. I'm getting my milk."

"Then get it," I said.

"I can and I will. And it will be for me and my cornflakes."

I turned to Fern. "Let's play Old Maid."

"Let's."

I pulled out the cards and Fern and I sat on the rug with our legs folded. Then I dealt cards to Fern and me, Fern and me, until we had our hands.

Vonetta turned on her heel.

That night, as the Apollo 11 spacecraft continued on its journey back to Earth, Uncle D came home from school and work at the mill. Vonetta didn't speak to him, but she watched him. Saw that he had nothing but his lunch pail, coffee thermos, and college books. She grunted hard and angrily and marched into the room.

"No milk?" I asked.

He slapped his head. "I knew I forgot something. Look, I'll go—"

"You'll go lie down, son," Big Ma said. "The world doesn't spin and stop on a bowl of cornflakes. And we'll be lucky the earth keeps spinning like it's supposed to— with men poking through space, hopping around on God's moon. Son, you been working and going to school. You go lie down."

When we walked over to Miss Trotter's the next day, Miss Trotter was quick to shoo us away. "Get on back." She muttered something about Ma Charles and said, "Don't you feel this cold in the air?"

I was sweating from tramping through fields and trees in the heat. The steamy, hot air.

Miss Trotter raised a finger to the air and nodded. "You don't feel this cold? Get back over the creek before you get caught in it."

"Caught in what?" I asked.

"The storm," JimmyTrotter said. He looked up.

"Dern astronauts, ripping through space, tearing holes here and everywhere."

Then Vonetta said in Ma Charles's voice, her tambourine-shaking voice, "Cast not thy rod through the clouds," and then added in Big Ma's voice, "A mercy, Lord."

"Hear that?" Miss Trotter said. "Even that old sister of mine knows a storm's coming. Don't know why she let you out. Now get going."

"Can I take the bike, cousin JT? You know I'll bring it back."

JT?

And he let her rename him with a shrug and a nod.

"Sure, cuz."

"Tell her," I said. "Like you told me since the day Papa and I came over. Come on, tell her."

"Tell her what?"

"'Call me JimmyTrotter or don't call me.'"

JimmyTrotter smiled. "JT's all right between Vonetta and me."

"See, meanie?" she said to me.

And she rode the bike while Fern and I skipped over the creek.

Maybe there was something to what Miss Trotter, Ma Charles, and Big Ma had to say about man sending things out of this earth poking holes in the sky, and having wrath hurled back down at him. When the astronauts broke through the atmosphere and splashed down in the Pacific, we were repaid with an electrical storm. Every outlet was unplugged from every socket and the house stayed dark, except for the lit candle in a few rooms, including ours.

Fern and I huddled together, and Vonetta, determined

to not huddle with us, stayed over in her own corner of the room.

I didn't care how mad Vonetta was. I started to miss her so I said, "Come over here with us."

"Yeah, meanie. Come over."

Vonetta didn't even bother to say no. She just wrapped herself in her blanket and turned her back to us.

"Be that way," I said.

"Be," Fern echoed.

We had electrical storms in Brooklyn but nothing to confirm God's anger. Blasts of white gold blazed through the dark, and we covered our ears to brace for the thunder. First the sound of the earth being cracked open like a walnut, followed by booms big enough to move the house.

Each time the lightning cracked and the thunder boomed, Fern and I hugged tighter. Surely, Vonetta would forget being angry and scoot our way so we could be scared together.

Black Pocahontas stayed wrapped in her blanket teepee pretending to be unafraid. I don't remember the thunder and lightning ending but through it all, we'd fallen asleep.

In the morning when I woke up, Vonetta was gone.

Gone

There was no Vonetta in the bathroom, only signs that she had just been there. Her face towel was damp and she'd left a fresh gob of toothpaste on the sink's porcelain. I stuck my head in every room in the house but there was no Vonetta. Boy, was she going to get it from me. I didn't care how angry she was with Fern and me. She knew better than to go marching over the creek walkway to be with her beloved Trotters.

But just to check that she was really gone, I ran out to the henhouse. No Vonetta. I looked up to the cradle of my pecan tree, expecting to see her grinning down to show me I wasn't the only one who could climb a tree, and then I was really angry at her. I felt myself breathing fast and heavily. Wait until she comes walking into the house. I'd make her sorry she left without telling me. Boy, would she be sorry.

I had been shaking my fist, thinking of all kinds of punishments for Vonetta. Then I stopped. Something about the side of the henhouse caught my attention. I looked for the something without really knowing what I was looking for. Then it came to me: Last night, before we went inside from having been over the creek, Vonetta had leaned the bike against the henhouse. The bike was the missing thing. The bike was gone.

From there I saw fresh bicycle tracks baked into the dirt. I followed them, expecting they'd lead me to the pines toward the creek, but they stopped at the road. She hadn't gone toward Miss Trotter's home. She was headed in the opposite direction!

A queasiness came over me and I felt weak-kneed. As sure as anger rose up in me, a sick feeling took it sliding back down. *My sister. My sister. My sister is gone.*

"Vonetta! VON-ET-TAAA!"

Big Ma came outside through the back in her house-dress and Mr. Lucas came out on his porch and leaned against the post.

"Delphine. What do you mean by this noise? Waking up the neighbors. Lord, here he comes." Big Ma started to pat her scarf and wig in place and fluff her housedress.

Mr. Lucas was on his way over. His walk was more

urgent than Big Ma's. He must have heard my panic when Big Ma could hear only noise. I tried to tell Big Ma Vonetta was missing but she could only fuss about Mr. Lucas coming and I had to yell at her to make her hear me.

"Quiet! Quiet, Big Ma. Quiet! PLEASE."

"Girl, who do you—"

"Vonetta's gone, Big Ma," I said quickly. "Vonetta took the bike. She's gone."

Big Ma shook her head to the contrary. "Gone, nothing! That child rode that bicycle across the creek to fool with her cousin and Miss Trotter."

"That's what I thought. But look! See the tire tracks, Big Ma? They're going the other way. To town."

Big Ma looked down at the dirt tracks. She saw where they were headed. I heard a small but deep moan seep from her. Big Ma stepped away from me and started turning in circles, wringing her hands. Mr. Lucas was there to catch her and make her stop turning in circles. But she pushed away from him and tried to gather herself. Even though she'd heard me and seen the tracks, she asked, "What do you mean, Delphine? What do you mean?"

"She's gone, Big Ma. She was mad all last night and took off this morning." This was bad. Worse than the sick I felt coming on. So bad Big Ma didn't threaten to beat the daylights out of Vonetta when she got home.

"Why was she mad, Delphine? And where could she've gone?" Mr. Lucas asked. "A child either runs away from something or runs off to where they want to be. Or to what they want to have."

I didn't answer the first question. Only the second, although I knew the answers to both. "Milk," I said. "She went to get milk."

"All right, all right," Mr. Lucas said calmly. "That's down the road, less than two miles from here. I'll jump in the truck—"

"Truck's gone," I said. "Uncle Darnell went to work early."

"Call over to Miss Trotter's," Big Ma said, finding herself. "Miss Trotter's got that old car."

"JimmyTrotter can't drive the station wagon," I said. "The sheriff said he better not drive it without a license."

"I don't care a fig about Davey Lee Charles," Big Ma said. "I'm going to get my grandbaby."

Mr. Lucas tried to calm Big Ma down but Big Ma couldn't be calmed. She spoke against the white man who was her cousin. And the law. And the Klan. Big Ma could not be calmed.

Mr. Lucas said, "You tell JimmyTrotter I said to drive the car over and I'll take it into town. Fastest way to get the car here. The sooner for the little one"—he meant Vonetta—"the better."

While he comforted Big Ma, I turned to go inside the house. I might have even taken a step. But a hand grabbed my arm and I stopped where I stood.

Mr. Lucas didn't say a word. Both he and Big Ma were frozen, not speaking, but looking off and upward. Big Ma's hands covered her mouth. I turned to the direction that Big Ma and Mr. Lucas's eyes were fixed. Overhead but in the distance, toward town, where Vonetta must have ridden that bicycle, half of the sky was bright, and pushing against the bright was a darker blue.

Darker blue, then gray. Or was it smoke? It was growing like a smoke cloud from the sky to the ground. It seemed alive, angry and moving.

My pecan tree leaves flickered toward it, even though the dark thing was far away. But it grew dark. Darker. Then we heard the sound of gunshots. At least ten in the air.

"The warning." Mr. Lucas's voice was even, the way cops talk to people standing on a ledge threatening to jump. "Go get your baby sister," he said to me and eased the grip on my arm. "I'll get Ma." He took Big Ma's hand from her mouth and said, "Ophelia, go down in the root cellar."

"But—"

"We got"—he paused and looked at the dark—"less than ten minutes. Go. Now."

Big Ma seemed dazed or hypnotized by the dark out there. She kept looking at it while she moved slowly down the root cellar. Then Mr. Lucas said, "Go, Ophelia. Now!"

I asked Mr. Lucas nothing. Just did what he said.

Picked up Fern, who was heavier than she looked, and started back toward the doors to the cellar. Mr. Lucas had Ma Charles wrapped in her blanket, half leading her, half carrying her. "No time. No time, Ma," he said. "No time."

We headed down the cellar. He turned to me and said, "Still have about six minutes. Maybe five. Let's grab all the hens we can. No time for the eggs."

"Caleb," Fern said.

I could feel the wind. The pecan tree leaves all swayed to one side. Caleb didn't have to be told where to go. As soon as I loosened him from his chain he trotted down the steps to the cellar. Mr. Lucas started grabbing hens and almost threw them down the cellar. I did the same, chasing, grabbing, and throwing them down. With clipped wings, they couldn't fly far but they could still fly a little. I didn't ask a thing. I just did what Mr. Lucas said. There was no time to think or ask. I didn't know what the dark was about, but it was growing darker and windier. I looked up at it. We were running from a dark monster. I could barely breathe with the wind whisking up and around my nose. The dark was far away but I could feel it pulling. The dirt on the ground kicked about, sweeping and stirring. And then Mr. Lucas grabbed my arm. Between us we had the last of the hens, and we went down into the cellar. He closed the metal door and took the iron bar and pushed it through the holes that linked one metal door to the other. It was pitch-black in the root cellar, and it smelled of chickens, potatoes, turnips, onions, dirt, and breath. Big Ma no longer asked for a mercy. Instead she called on "Jesus! Jesus! Jesus!" over and over without stopping.

The chickens hopping everywhere in the dark were too much for Fern. "Get away, hens!" she cried out. "Get away!"

Caleb bayed and Ma Charles told him to hush but Caleb kept making his noise and the chickens squawked on and on.

"It could shift at the last second," Mr. Lucas said.

"Maybe it shifted before . . . Vonetta . . ."

"We'll just hold on," Mr. Lucas said, not letting me finish, and that was best. "We'll just hold on."

I grabbed Fern, and Fern held on to me and Caleb.

Then everything shook. I kept my eyes closed but I could hear the noise of things flying, crashing, falling, knocking against other things. Glass breaking. Rain shooting. Horrible, horrible noises.

"Jesus! Jesus! Jesus!"

The storm door clanked fiercely like murderers were at the door, tugging and shaking to break in. Chickens squawked something terrible.

Through it all, Fern cried out for Vonetta. "Vonetta! Vonetta! Where's Vonetta?" I couldn't answer her. I could only cry. We were all in there crying. Big Ma, Ma Charles. Even Caleb.

Mr. Lucas spoke first. He put a name to the darkening,

the shaking in the air and in the ground and why every-thing around us was flying. Breaking. Slamming. Falling. "Tornado!" Mr. Lucas yelled. "Tornado's passing."

I couldn't see what was outside but I felt it pounding on the root cellar door. I heard it tossing things about. And I knew. I knew my sister was out there. Out there pedaling on a bike. An old bicycle was all she had out there. My sister was out there.

Blue Sky

Caleb was the first to bound up the steps and out into the light when Mr. Lucas undid the iron bar and together we heaved the root cellar doors open. The sky looked as if it hadn't blackened in the first place. Blue. Pretty. We hadn't even spent fifteen minutes down in the cellar. People say "unreal" as an expression, but this was truly unreal. For all the banging, crashing, and whomping we heard while we were down below, the sky had the nerve to be a beautiful shade of blue.

We stepped out from the dark into what was now an altogether different place. No one could speak. I turned around and around in disbelief. In less than fifteen minutes everything except the house had been turned upside down. Smashed eggs. Straw and feed everywhere. No henhouse. Just planks and splinters. No chicken run. Just swept away. Caleb's house was knocked over on its side but it was still one whole house. One of the metal poles for the clothesline leaned while the other had been uprooted and thrown. The clothesline itself, with white sheets still pinned to it, was nowhere to be seen. The cradling branches of my pecan tree had been snapped clean off but the tree still stood. The telephone poles stood firm, but the pines, both narrow and thick, had fallen, like soldiers in ugly army green had been shot up in the road. Just unreal.

"Thank you, Jesus!" Big Ma shouted in spite of the horrific unreal every which way we looked. "House is still standing."

"Only one window broken but not a shingle loose," Ma Charles said. "Thank you, Jesus!"

"Good storm windows," Mr. Lucas said. It was how he said it that I knew he was responsible for those storm windows.

And then we turned to Mr. Lucas's house. The pillar posts on both sides had snapped in two and the roof had caved in. A pine tree had fallen through the roof. Unreal.

"Son, oh son, oh son," Ma Charles said, her voice wobbly with true sorrow.

"Jesus, Jesus, Jesus." Big Ma took and squeezed Mr. Lucas's hand.

Mr. Lucas said, "Let's keep on praising Him. I've seen worse." As if they were standing before a miracle, my great-grandmother, my grandmother, and Mr. Lucas continued praising the Lord like they were in church. But we weren't in church. We were standing in the unreal. Topsy-turvy, broken, and scattered.

How could they praise Him? How could they thank Him? As sure as I stood and saw it all, the busted hen-house and smashed eggs, the split-up pecan tree, its parts blown away, Mr. Lucas's house half standing and half fallen, hundred-year-old pine trees snapped like twigs, I knew what that tornado could do to my little sister on a bicycle. I knew she had no chance out there.

Fern went running into the house and I went after her. She shouted, "VONETTA! VONETTA!" expecting Vonetta to appear from underneath the bed with her hands on her narrow hips. She called into each room, "Vonetta! Vonetta!" like she didn't want it to be true about Vonetta. That she was gone. Gone for good.

I caught her. Then I said it. "She's gone, Fern."

"Where?"

"Out there. In the tornado."

"I want Vonetta!" she screamed at me.

"We all want her."

"You don't."

"I do."

"No, you don't. You're mean to Vonetta. You pick on her."

"Because she picks on you."

"Because you pick on her!" she shouted at me. "Stop being mean, Delphine. Stop being so mean and bossy."

Fern didn't know what she was saying. I understood that. She was upset. That storm shook us all and we were missing Vonetta. I couldn't be mad at her for what she said. We were all in shock and sick about Vonetta.

I reached out to shoulder-hug her but she pushed against me and out of my arms and ran to Ma Charles.

Mr. Lucas had Big Ma turn the lights and water on and off. On and off. Then she picked up the phone for an outside line.

"Call over to Miss Trotter," he said. "See if she's there."

I said, "The bicycle tracks ran—"

"I know, Delphine," he said. "But let's check first and see if they're all right."

Big Ma held up the phone's receiver to me and I took it.

I dialed Miss Trotter's number, both hoping but also knowing not to hope. I had seen the tire tracks leading to the road before the wind came and scattered the last trace of Vonetta. I knew she was on her way to town for a bottle of milk.

"Is it ringing?" Ma Charles asked. "Lord, let there be ringing." And they started praying and praising the Lord for a phone line. But the line rang funny. Different.

"I don't think their phone works," I said.

"I'll go over there to check on them," Mr. Lucas said.

"You'll go to town to see about Vonetta," Ma Charles

said. "Darnell will go across the creek to see about the Trotters."

"I can go," I said.

"You'll go nowhere," Big Ma said. "Dangerous as it is."

"Your grandmother's right," Mr. Lucas said. "Timber can fall any which way, and who knows if the wooden crossing's steady or standing." He looked to Big Ma and said, "I'll go on toward town on foot."

"Just bring her back," Big Ma told him.

"I'm going to try," he said.

"Bring her back," she said again. "Bring her back, Elijah. I can't rest until she comes through that door. My heart, Elijah. My heart's beating so. I can't rest till she's home."

"Darnell will be here soon," Mr. Lucas said.

I couldn't stay there inside and followed after Mr. Lucas. "I'll go with you," I said.

"No, Delphine. Stay here with your grandmothers and your sister. I need you to start piling that henhouse wood. Gather up what straw you can. Rake the yard for nails. Glass, too. Can't let the chickens up out of the cellar until the ground's safe. When you're done here, I'll need you to help me clear my yard."

I didn't want to do any of those things but "Yes, sir," fell out of my mouth nice and easy.

Big Ma shouted to Mr. Lucas to be careful. He waved to her and was on his way.

The Call

"Daughter, call your father."

I was the only one in the kitchen with Ma Charles but I couldn't believe she meant me. That I had to be the one to make the phone call. Even though Big Ma said she couldn't rest, she was lying down in the other room. It was just as well. Her face was covered in sweat and she didn't look good.

I still asked, "Shouldn't Big Ma call Papa?"

"Don't question me, daughter. Pick up this phone and dial that number. Your father needs to know."

What do I tell him? What do I say?

"Come on, daughter. That's your father. Your sister. Make the call."

I didn't want to do it. I shouldn't have to. I shouldn't have to. But the phone was in my hand and my great-grandmother stared into me with no intention of repeating herself.

I knew Pa's number in the dark. My finger hooked into the first circle on the dial and my fingers pulled around, dialing for a long-distance line, the area code, followed by "AT7" and the last four digits. I thought I would be unsteady, shaky, and sobbing. Unable to speak. I thought all the tears and nausea pooling in me would come up and I'd choke when he picked up the receiver and I had to speak. But when the phone rang, and the line clicked when he picked up the phone, and his voice said, "Hello," my mouth opened and I spoke calmly. "Papa. Papa."

Pa's voice didn't leap toward mine, asking me how my sisters and I were making out and such. Instead, he waited. Waited for me to speak. He knew. He knew. My stomach knotted something awful. He knew I didn't call with good news. Then he said, "Yes, Delphine." His voice was so calm. So steady. Full of stillness and waiting.

"Vonetta is lost. Vonetta got lost in the tornado."

No sound. Then a terrible sound. A bear caught in a trap. His growl and moan went through me and made me queasy. In the background I heard Mrs. saying, "Honey, honey," over and over.

Her voice came through the receiver. Warm. Steady. "Delphine." She said it again, "Delphine," because I didn't answer. I couldn't. "Tell me, Delphine. Tell me what's going on." Papa was crying in the background, loud, like I never heard before. He couldn't tell her.

I finally spoke into the phone. "Vonetta got lost in the tornado. Vonetta's gone."

I didn't say the other thing although I thought it. I didn't say what I knew Papa heard although I didn't use that word. I couldn't use that word.

"Delphine . . ." She didn't say how horrible it was or start saying, "No! No!" so I'd have to say it again. Mrs. said, "Oh, Delphine, Delphine," gently. I could hear my father, wounded in the background. "Delphine, Delphine," she said. "Are you all right?"

I said, "Yes," but that wasn't true.

"Okay. Let me speak to your grandmother."

"I can't. I mean, she can't. She's . . . she's . . ."

"It's all right, Delphine. We'll be there tomorrow."

And she said love words to me and I took them knowing I didn't deserve them. Then we said good-bye.

Ma Charles didn't ask me what Papa said. Instead she said, "Now call your mother."

I couldn't tell her my mother was out of reach. That she didn't have a phone. I didn't know how to get my mother to a telephone. Or know if she would come to a telephone just because I called. I didn't know how to explain Cecile to my great-grandmother and that she wasn't the type to stop her work or disturb her peace of mind and come because I asked her to.

"Well?" Ma Charles said. "That's her blood. Her child. She has to know. Go on, daughter. Call her."

I made a plan in my head. I dialed "0." I stretched my voice from twelve to twenty-one and said, "Operator, I need the number for Ming's in Oakland on Magnolia." The operator still asked for my mama and I said, "I'm trying to reach my mama," although that was the last thing I'd call Cecile to her face. "It's an emergency."

The operator said, "Little girl, the telephone isn't a plaything," and hung up.

The dial tone was loud. Ma Charles said, "Try it again, daughter." My great-grandmother didn't want any of my excuses. Even if it was out of my hands. I dialed "0" and waited.

"It's an emergency, operator," I said. "It's about the tornado and I have to reach my mother."

"What city?" the voice said. A different operator.

"Oakland." I tried to sound grown and sure. I didn't want her to call me a little girl. "My mother's at Ming's Chinese Takeout on Magnolia Street." My mother wasn't really there, but Mean Lady Ming would remember me from last summer and she'd know how to get word to my mother. I spoke firmly and hoped my stretching the truth would get the call put through, but the operator was saying something about prank phone calls so loud that Ma

Charles could hear her questioning the call.

"Gimme that telephone," Ma Charles said, and I handed the receiver to her. She cleared her throat. "Put the call through for my great-granddaughter" was all she said and handed the phone back to me as if that was enough.

It was. The operator read off the numbers for Ming's Chinese Takeout on Magnolia and said, "Please hold while I connect you."

"Takeout. What you want?"

"Miss Ming?" I spoke timidly, as if I was standing at her counter for the first time.

"Hello?"

"Miss Ming," I said.

She fussed at me to stop playing on the phone. She had a business to run.

"No, Miss Ming. It's Delphine. Cecile's daughter."

"Delphine, Delphine." It took repeating my name for her to remember me from last summer.

"My mother. It's an emergency. I need her to call me."

She fussed that she couldn't leave the store, and I said, "Please, Miss Ming. It's bad. It's bad and I need her." I begged and begged her to write down the number. Then I heard Big Ma say, "Who you calling?" But I said to Miss Ming, "Please, Miss Ming. Please. Emergency." Then she said, "Okay, okay, Delphine," and hung up.

"Who you calling?"

Ma Charles stood up. "I told her to call her mother."

I was grateful to have my great-grandmother next to me, looking clear-eyed and ready for a fight.

"Far's I'm concerned, those girls don't have a mother."

"Whether you think so or not, she and the other two have a mother, and their mother should know." She drummed her finger against the tabletop hard with every point she made.

"Hmp."

"We don't teach a child to dishonor her mother or father. Not in this house." Then Ma Charles told me to go and get her shawl from her room. What next she had to tell Big Ma was not for my ears and I scooted out of there.

Over the next few hours, my tears hadn't dried, nor had my stomach settled. But I kept my ears open, waiting. Hoping the phone would ring soon. And also not wanting it to ring. Not wanting to tell Cecile.

Then one ring. One shrill ring was all it took to get me into the kitchen. I grabbed the receiver on the second ring.

"Cecile," I said. I knew it was her.

"I don't like people knocking on my door," she told me. My mouth went dry.

"Cecile," I said.

"You got the Woods boy knocking on my door, dragging me out of my house. Delphine, you know better.

There's nothing you have to tell me that calls for all of that."

If I didn't say it fast, plain, and clear, she'd hang up on me and write me a letter-poem telling me about myself. So I said it. "Vonetta left the house this morning. She's lost in the tornado. We can't find her."

I waited. And waited. And waited. Next came a click. Then the moan of the dial tone.

I felt breathing. Fast, heavy breathing. Big Ma.

"What she say?" Ma Charles asked.

I could barely look at them. "She didn't say anything. She . . ." I didn't want to tell them but there was no hiding it. "She hung up."

Big Ma clapped her hands hard. One hard clap. "What did I say? What did I tell you?" She was angry with me and pleased with herself for having Cecile pegged right.

"Now—"

Big Ma cut her mother off. "Mama. You don't know what that woman did to them. Ripped herself out from under them and ran off to parts unknown. You don't know how she tore my son's heart clean out of his chest. She didn't mother them then, can't mother them now. Too busy writing words on the wall or whatever she calls herself doing."

After my grandmother pointed her finger and hollered at her own mother, she turned to me. "I told you and told you about Cecile, but you wouldn't take the truth from my mouth. You wouldn't take the gospel truth from the one who raised you. And now you've seen and heard it for yourself. As far as I'm concerned, you don't have a mother. And don't you speak her name or about her in this lifetime. Ever!"

I felt like I was being knocked down again and again and again, but when I turned, I fell into my uncle's arms. "Go 'head, cry, Delphine," he whispered, rocking me like I was a little girl. "We're all crying."

TaRaNada

A full day hadn't passed by, but Vonetta's absence lingered in every corner of the house. Everywhere I turned was a space Vonetta had been in that was now left empty. I was glad Mr. Lucas had given me something to do, although it didn't take long to gather the planks of broken wood from the henhouse and the baby dresser drawers that were once the hens' nesting boxes. They made a small, splintery pile of wood that couldn't be used for anything else. It was in raking the yard, searching for nails and glass pieces blown over from Mr. Lucas's house, that gave my eyes a downward place to look. For that I was glad. I searched and searched for broken bits while I missed Vonetta and missed Fern and hated my mother and thought of what Fern had yelled at me and dreaded seeing my father's face but wanted him here with me at the same time.

Uncle Darnell would soon go over the creek to see about the Trotters. When I asked to go with him he said, "We'll see," which I hoped was a strong maybe. I wanted to see how JimmyTrotter and Miss Trotter were, but at the same time, I was afraid of what I might see. Mr. Lucas's house was sturdy and Miss Trotter's house was old. Its floorboards spoke with every step we took whenever we were inside the house. She kept everything as it was when her father had lived with her and Ella Pearl. According to my cousin, Mr. Lucas had made offers to "gird up the house's foundation" over the years, but Miss Trotter had always told JimmyTrotter the house was fine as it was. She didn't want anyone to touch what her father had made.

I decided I'd rather be anywhere but here, even if I had to see what I didn't want to see.

I scratched and clawed at the ground, waiting for Uncle Darnell to take me with him. On television they never say the person's name when there is a missing person and that person is found. Instead, they say, "The body has been found," because the body is all that is left. But if she was found, still inside her body, still alive, they'd say, "We found the little girl. We found Vonetta Gaither."

I didn't want to believe it. Any of it. Not that it was my

fault, like Fern said. Not that my sister was gone. Not that Vonetta was gone for good. I didn't want anyone to say, "We found the body."

I kept my head down. I raked and clawed.

Caleb started up his noise, louder than his usual dog song. I stopped tearing up the ground with the rake and instead combed it softly, waiting for our visitor to come into view. Caleb could cry and carry on long before a stranger or a hungry fox could be seen. My heart quickened, wanting to hope. He didn't only sing out for strangers. He sang when the visitor was someone he knew. Like Vonetta. I kept the rake going but I stopped breathing.

Finally, the moving car showed itself—the sheriff's black-and-white car. It turned off the tree-blocked road and jostled through the field of dandelions and wildflowers. I searched the car, hoping to see my sister. I saw something besides the sheriff, but it wasn't my sister. The car was now up on the grass but it didn't come any closer. The sheriff got out, then opened the passenger door and a bloodhound jumped out. Caleb pulled at his chain and pitched a fuss, so I let him off of his chain and he was on Sheriff Charles in no time, jumping, licking, and baying like a pup. The two dogs scampered about excitedly, glad to see each other. Still excited, Caleb nipped at the sheriff's pants leg but the sheriff didn't look down at Caleb or pet him. He just flung Caleb off of him, kicking out his leg once, and the two dogs went back to playing with each other while the sheriff trudged up to the house.

As he approached I realized that he was more Big Ma and Mr. Lucas's age. Maybe a little younger. He was broad from shoulder to belly and then narrow from the hip—where his holster sat—down to his boots. I felt no need to give the greeting Big Ma had taught my sisters and me to give all grown folk, especially to white folk. I knew who he was. I knew he wore a white sheet when he wasn't wearing his badge.

It made him no difference whether I spoke to him or not. He tapped on the screen door with the back of his hand and called out, "'Phelia! You there? Mama? It's Davey Lee."

Uncle Darnell met him at the door and opened it wide. I thought he did that to be the man of the house and stand up to the Klan—but my uncle opened the door wide and shook the sheriff's hand. *Shook his hand.* And brought him inside my great-grandmother's house.

I got up to the porch to see and hear through the screen door. Why was he here if he didn't have my sister—and who did he think he was, calling Ma Charles "Mama"? I was mad enough to scream just when I thought I'd been wrung out numb. *The Klan was in my great-grandmother's house. My uncle shook his hand.* Unreal. Crazy unreal. Yet I couldn't take myself away.

Fern was glued to Ma Charles the way she should have been glued to me. The sheriff looked down at Fern and

212

then said to Ma Charles, "Should have figured those were yours."

Ma Charles nodded. "They're mine. All three."

"When was the last you seen her?" he asked.

Big Ma said, "Supper last night. Just before the thundering and lightning started. The kids went to their beds early. Stayed in their room."

"No chance she went out in the electrical storm last night?"

"No," Fern said. And everyone turned to her in a kind of shock because Fern said very little. "She stayed on her side of the room and me and Delphine stayed on our side. But we all went to bed." Then she added, "Vonetta snores. Loud. She kept me awake with her snoring. I thought she was snoring loud to get back at Delphine and me because we didn't let her play Old Maid with us."

He nodded to that and asked Big Ma for a recent photograph, and she told Fern to go in her room and get her church purse. Fern hurried off and returned with the black bag. Big Ma took out her wallet and from there she carefully pulled out a small picture. A school picture.

The sheriff looked at the picture once, shook his head, probably at Vonetta's proud-of-herself grin. He probably thought no black girl had the right to be that proud, but there she was, being Vonetta in a photo.

"You know not to hope, 'Phelia," the sheriff said. "Taranada"—that was exactly how he said it, with four

213

syllables, all *A*'s—"wasn't the worst, but I tell you one thing. It was bad enough to toss that Negro rag doll clear 'cross the county, out of this lifetime."

Mr. Lucas had to catch Big Ma and Uncle Darnell said, "Hey, man. You didn't have to say that."

The sheriff said, "Better the truth than a fairy tale."

"We're not asking you for no fairy tale," Ma Charles said. "We're asking you to do what the sheriff's supposed to do. We're asking you to find our lost child."

"Yes, Mama," the sheriff said.

I hated that he called her that, but she said, "Just go find her, son. Go find her." *Son.* My great-grandmother called the Klan *son.*

"All right then, Mama," he said. He turned to Uncle Darnell and said, "I need a piece of her clothing. Something she wore yesterday. Pj's, maybe."

Fern then ran off again and returned with Vonetta's nightie. But she didn't hand it over to the sheriff. She gave it to Ma Charles, and Ma Charles lifted her hand for the sheriff to lean over and take it.

I got away from the door.

He called his dog and the dog trotted up to his boots. Caleb followed. He knelt and gave the nighties to his dog to sniff. "Scent, boy. Scent." Both dogs went at it. Caleb, sniffing and baying loud and crazy. "Where she, boy? Where that li'l Negro child?"

Something about the way he said it. *Negro.* Like he was

used to saying the other word. The bad word.

"Darnell! Darnell!" he shouted, sounding more like an army sergeant giving orders than a sheriff. When Uncle Darnell came out, the sheriff said, "We got a scent."

"I'm coming," my uncle told the sheriff.

"Well, come on, then."

"Can I go?" I asked. I don't know what made me ask. I didn't want to be near that Ku Klux Klansman.

I was asking my uncle but the sheriff said, "Naw. This is a manhunt. Sheriff business."

Then Uncle Darnell said, "Stay here."

They leashed up both dogs and set off down the road and into the pines, the dogs baying and pulling. I put the rake down and sat on the porch. I looked to the pines, hoping.

I heard both dogs before I saw them. "They're coming!" I yelled to Big Ma, Ma Charles, and Fern. "They're coming!"

I wanted to see Uncle Darnell carrying Vonetta but when we finally saw them, it was Uncle D, the sheriff, and the two bloodhounds.

"We found the bicycle," the sheriff said. "Up a tree in ten pieces."

"A mercy, Lord. A mercy, a mercy."

"But we didn't find the body."

"She's not the body!" I screamed at him. "She's Vonetta."

Big Ma grabbed me by the arm. "Girl, you shut your

mouth. You hear me? You just shut your mouth."

Uncle D pulled me in to him.

The sheriff went on. "Scent got cold. Taranada might have blown her anywhere. The body could be up in one them trees."

I was glad when Sheriff Charles had finally left. I hoped he would find Vonetta, and I hoped he wouldn't.

Caleb could not be calmed. Once he sniffed that old sheriff and his brother and Vonetta's scent from the nightie, there was no quieting him down. I put his chain back on him and tied him up good, but Caleb kept sniffing and pulling. Pulling after the sheriff's car.

I knew they used dogs. The sheriffs down here. I knew this from our summer at the People's Center. I had seen old photographs of cops siccing dogs on people. Black people. And college students. Now the sheriff would use the dog to find where the tornado had blown Vonetta.

Caleb wouldn't stop singing his dog song. Missing his hound-dog brother and maybe even the sheriff. "Hush, Caleb," I said. "Hush that noise." But he wouldn't hear me. He bayed louder and louder and then kept it to a loud, one-note song.

When I looked up I saw what he was barking at. I saw it but I could barely believe it. I didn't know who to call first so I yelled, "Everyone! Come see! Come see!"

Sister

My hand flew to my mouth. My eyes saw it but my mind spun in disbelieving circles. The closer they came out of the pines and into the field and toward the grass, the more real it became. Fern, Uncle Darnell, Mr. Lucas, Big Ma, and Ma Charles came out to the porch to see the commotion. I took off running to the pines. I ran to Miss Trotter, JimmyTrotter, Sophie, and Butter. The sight of them sent me racing on the inside! Miss Trotter on foot, holding on to the cane Ma Charles had given her. JimmyTrotter leading the cows. Miss Trotter's wooden chair strapped to Sophie's back. What a sight! What a sight! I jumped up as I ran. I was the first to get there, winded, hugging, and crying. So glad to see them. So glad. It was the only good thing that had happened this day.

"Miss Trotter! Miss Trotter! You're here! You're here! At last!"

"As sure as you're born," Miss Trotter said. "As sure as you're born." She had a grip on that cane in one hand and the picture of her parents in the other. Both she and JimmyTrotter carried knapsacks on their backs, his bigger than hers, but it looked like they carried all that they had left. Uncle Darnell and I helped them out of their bags and took them. Miss Trotter was winded after having walked the distance, and her skirt was wet from about her knee to her feet. Fern petted Sophie and Butter and told them not to be afraid of Caleb. Caleb kept up his dog song. Big Ma praised the Lord and started to fuss over Miss Trotter. Mr. Lucas took a rope from JimmyTrotter and led the cows up to the house.

"You're wet, Auntie," Big Ma said. "You'll catch your death."

"Death ain't caught me by the ankle yet," Miss Trotter said, but she was shivering. "Guess I keep right on stepping."

"The tornado destroyed the walkway so we went through the water," JimmyTrotter said. "Had to go all the way down to the shallows. Cows didn't like it much, but we're here." And Miss Trotter started to hum a song I knew: "Wading in the Water."

By this time Ma Charles was making her way down

to us. Miss Trotter stopped humming and fussing once she caught sight of her ambling toward us all. Big Ma fussed at Mr. Lucas to "help Ma," and Ma Charles refused Mr. Lucas's hand when he tried to help her. I figured she didn't want her sister to see she wasn't as steady as she once was.

Sophie mooed, which sparked Butter mooing, and Caleb had never quite stopped crying his dog song. It just got louder. But not one of us spoke a word. In fact, Big Ma placed her hand over Mr. Lucas's lips to keep him from speaking. Then Miss Trotter, digging that cane in the ground with each step, made her way to Ma Charles.

"Sister," one called out.

"Sister," the other called out.

JimmyTrotter described everything. How the tornado came their way and took down half of the barn and most of the house. That they had only two minutes to get to the crawl space under the house and that Miss Trotter wouldn't go without Mama and Papa so JimmyTrotter had to get the photograph from the mantel.

"It's all just kindling," Miss Trotter said. "'Cept for Papa's chair. Tornado threw it good, but JimmyTrotter found it up a tree."

"I didn't think I'd get it down, but here it is."

Mr. Lucas offered to take a look at it and make sure it

was sturdy but Miss Trotter wouldn't let him touch her father's chair.

"House shaking on top of us, this way and that," Miss Trotter said. "The wind was having its way. Wasn't nothing we could do but pray."

"Prayer works," Ma Charles said.

"Didn't I say don't go poking in the sky?"

"Through God's heavens," Ma Charles said. "You must have heard me saying it. Tell 'em," Ma Charles said to me. It seemed the first time anyone had said anything at all to me. All I could do was nod my head yes and remember that I still had to face my father. In the middle of this one good thing, my belly started to ache.

"I knew it was trouble when I felt that air, sister."

"Cold here," Ma Charles said.

"And heat stirring there," the other finished. "It's all that stirring up. Sending men into space and hurling them back down. Poking holes where they need not poke holes."

"Electric storm is the ma and pa," one said.

"And the tornado is its wayward child," the other said.

"There wasn't a finer teacher than Miss Rice."

"Surely and truly," the other said.

"It's a wonder we still have Sophie and Butter," Jimmy-Trotter said. "You wouldn't know the barn to see it."

"What barn? Just a pile of sticks. House too. Kindling."

"Like the henhouse!" Fern cried.

Everyone spoke on about the tornado. Things brought

down. Some homes standing. Some split apart into nothingness. But I stayed silent, like I didn't have a right to the
family sounds. I was at the table but I was watching. On
the outside.

"What is a barn, or a henhouse?" Miss Trotter said.
"What are two cows? I'd give those cows and more to see
my sister with all her greats."

And then they began to pray for Vonetta. Moan for her.
Cry for her.

"My line had sons. Nothing but sons," Miss Trotter said.
"It was all we could do to keep the Trotter name going
for Papa."

Then Ma Charles said, "My line has daughters. The
names add on, but we keep the bloodline going."

"I've got—" Miss Trotter started.

"Each other," Big Ma said, before they could get a
squabble started.

One said, "Sister."

The other said, "Sister."

Things went well between them until one said, "Mrs.
Hazzard."

Then the other said, "Massa Charles's property," and I
thought they would never stop.

Big Ma said, "You two are worse than those three ever
were."

But there were only two of us now. Two. Big Ma started
to cry. And then Fern and I started. Mr. Lucas said, "Come

on, Ophelia. I'll take you to your room. You need to rest."

Then Ma Charles said, "You stay here, son. Where I can see you."

And Miss Trotter said, "Young folk."

And my great-grandmother agreed. "Young'ns."

ThRee Dog Night

After all of the eating, talking, praying, and being among
family, the house finally fell quiet. No one paid Caleb any
mind, baying and carrying on into the night. He hadn't
been the same since Sheriff Charles gave him Vonetta's
nightie to sniff. He had "the scent" and kept pulling at his
chain and baying.

The churning of things both bad and unknown kept
me awake. It was mostly being in our room. Feeling the
before and the now in every corner. Caleb's noise didn't
help any more than knowing my father must have driven
the Wildcat as far as Virginia by now. Or North Carolina.

All I had wanted was to have every single one of us
under one roof. Now, with so many of us, and Papa and

Mrs. coming, I felt like I couldn't breathe. I crept by Mr. Lucas, who was asleep on the sofa, and picked my way through my uncle and cousin camped out on the living room floor. I hoped the floorboards wouldn't give me away. Thanks to Mr. Lucas, our floors didn't creak as much as Miss Trotter's old wooden floors. Uncle Darnell turned over and I froze at the door, but neither he, JimmyTrotter, nor Mr. Lucas woke up.

I stepped out on the porch in my bare feet. Caleb wouldn't stop barking. His chain never bothered him before. He had been content to sit in the sun and watch the chickens scratching around in the chicken run. But now he tugged at the pole, spiked down into the ground extra hard by Mr. Lucas.

I listened to him and heard something familiar in his song. It was more than Caleb wanting to be free of his chains. He made the same sounds as when Sheriff Charles came riding up in his police car and again when Miss Trotter, JimmyTrotter, Sophie, and Butter came from out of the pines. I never thought about a meaning behind Caleb's baying. Only that he made his noise. But now I could hear that Caleb's third dog song—two during daylight and one at night—was a song to announce an arrival.

Still, I said, "Hush, boy."

Caleb wouldn't hush. He pulled at his chain and sang louder.

I turned on the porch light. I saw movement in the

dark. A person approaching. My eyes combed through the dark for a better look but all I could see was the figure that was now coming through the field and moving toward the house.

I didn't move. I only watched. The dog kept crying as the figure came closer. Then she was upon me. It was my mother. Cecile.

She hadn't even gotten fully to the porch but she was already speaking. "They find Vonetta?"

I had to stop myself from saying, "No, ma'am," knowing my mother wouldn't like that southern talk. I said, "No, Cecile. They didn't find her."

"Your father here?"

"Not yet," I said. I wanted to hug my mother but she didn't open herself to let me. So I stayed where I was. All she wanted from me were answers, so I gave what I had. "Uncle Darnell said the way Papa drives, he and Mrs. will be here just after noon."

"Mrs.?"

"Pa's . . . wife."

"Her name is Marva," Cecile said flatly.

"Yes, ma'am." It slipped out. I knew right there my mother hated the South in me. She cut me up with her glare.

Then Uncle Darnell came to the door and pushed it open. "Sis!"

She clomped past me—her footsteps heavy, like I

remembered, and hugged his neck so hard. They stood there wrapped in each other. Her eyes shut tight. I heard her say to him, "I never meant to leave you." Something she'd never said to me or my sisters.

Then he spoke into her neck. "I know, sis."

"I just couldn't stay," she told him.

He said, "I know."

I was right there but on the outside. It didn't seem real. My mother, wild-eyed and tired, suddenly here. Close enough to touch, although she didn't reach out to me or let me touch her. But I smelled the coconut oil in her hair and the sweat of someone who'd been marching ten miles. When I thought I had the right to hate her, she was there. Right there. But not for me to touch. Except for the big drawstring bag slung around her shoulder that hit me when she went to hug Uncle Darnell. The bag was soft and full, its punch dull against my side. It was a bag I knew she'd made of old clothes.

My mother stomped on the welcome mat to shake the dirt from her boots and went inside with Uncle Darnell. I stayed outside with Caleb, who was now back to baying and pulling at his chain.

I stayed out on the porch all night and didn't slip back inside until nearly daybreak. Cecile slept in the living room next to Uncle Darnell as if they had fallen asleep talking. Mr. Lucas now lay on his back. But JimmyTrotter had moved from his spot. I walked through the living room into the kitchen and out the back screen door. There was JimmyTrotter with Sophie and Butter.

He had one of Big Ma's mixing bowls on the ground and sat at Sophie's side. "Come on, girl. Come on, Sophie."

I sat at his side. "Maybe she can't."

"I'm hoping she can," JimmyTrotter said. "It's too early for her to be dry. We don't have much use for a milk cow that don't milk."

"Don't let Fern hear you say that."

He gave a weak smile. "I don't know. Maybe I'll try breeding her in a few months. Maybe she'll give me a dairy cow. We sure haven't been lucky lately. Both Butter and Sophie gave us bulls." He shrugged. "Couldn't keep them."

Even as he spoke, I didn't quite believe him about breeding Sophie to try for another milk cow. I think he said those things because they were hopeful things. I think he said those things for me.

"Who's that woman?" he asked.

"Cecile," I said.

"Cecile, as in your mama? All the way from Los Angeles?"

"Oakland."

"Same difference from where I'm sitting." He looked up at the sky. "She flew to get here. A red-eye from Oakland to Montgomery, I'll bet. I'm figuring on a Boeing 707 or a DC-8. You know they're coming out with commercial planes almost as fast as the speed of sound. Wouldn't mind flying one of those."

"Is that so?"

He gave up on milking and set the mixing bowl aside. He kept looking to the sky. "My model planes are all smashed," he said. "If only I could have saved the Warhawk—or my brother's bomber. I only had time enough to grab Miss Trotter and the picture. Had to get the picture. She wouldn't move without her mama and papa."

"Onchee," I said.

"Onchee is right."

I told him I was sorry about his model planes when I wasn't. A model plane wasn't a sister, but JimmyTrotter was the only one speaking to me. And he had lost a brother, a mother, a father, and a grandmother. All at once. He knew.

"Wanted that Cessna, too. Last kit my daddy bought me." He wasn't really speaking to me. Just talking into the sky. "All of them gone."

Out of the blue I said, "It's not my fault."

"I didn't say it was."

"She's my sister. I want her back."

"I know, Delphine." Then we said nothing for a while.

"You must be glad to have your mama here," he said. "Even as sad as things are."

I knew from that he didn't believe we'd get Vonetta

back but I couldn't think that way.

"Cecile's not a mama," I told him, but not angry or snippy. I was just stating a fact.

"What do you mean?"

"She's Cecile. That's all."

He nodded like he understood, but I knew he didn't. We'd never run out of things to talk about before but we hardly had anything to say to each other now. I figured he'd stop talking to me like everyone else. And then Papa would be here and it would get worse before it got better. And it might never get better.

JimmyTrotter got up from his stool and I stood with him.

"Darnell's going back with me to pick through what's left. Maybe we can find some photos or something."

"I'll come too. I can help."

"Cousin Del, you don't want to see the house. Tornado hit us hard. Radio says it was a two but I think it was a level three."

There it was. His nice way of saying, *Leave me alone. I don't want you around.* I said, "Cousin, I just don't get it." He waited for me to finish. "Why did it take down your house and Mr. Lucas's house? Why is ours still standing?"

JimmyTrotter shrugged. "House is here. But you still got hit. Hard."

You Are the Hill

I followed Cecile as she walked inside each room looking for Big Ma. When she found her she said, "Mrs. Gaither. I'm here." I expected Big Ma to be thrown for a loop or to jump out of her skin. There was no reaction from Big Ma, as far as I could see. She cocked her head, crossed her arms, and said, "I see that."

There were no more words between them so I led my mother to the room that Ma Charles and Miss Trotter now shared. I said, "Ma Charles, Miss Trotter, this is our mother, Cecile."

Cecile said, "If it was a good morning, I'd wish you both a good one. Instead, I wish you're both well."

"Daughter!" Ma Charles cried. "Come over here so we can look at you."

My mother walked up to them like she was home.

"Didn't have to tell us who she is," Miss Trotter said. "That's your face, right there," she said to me. "The other ones, too. But that's you."

It was the one small burst of pleasure I felt, even though my mother and I hadn't hugged or really spoken to each other. Not really.

"Wake up, Fern."

"No."

"Wake up, Fern."

She kept her eyes shut. "Is Vonetta here?"

I said a soft no. She slumped over to give me her back.

"Wake up, Fern."

She pretended to be asleep.

"Little girl. Get out of that bed."

Fern sprang up and screamed. She ran to Cecile, bulling her head into Cecile's belly like she was trying to get back inside of her. Cecile picked her up and hugged her tight and swung her around.

I wanted nothing more than to be invited in, but I stayed where I was. I never knew I could feel so awful, so jealous, but I couldn't make those feelings go away.

Cecile put Fern down on the bed, sat with her, and told her she wasn't leaving until we found Vonetta. I almost backed out of the room but Cecile said, "Don't go nowhere," and continued talking to Fern. Now she faced me. "All right," Cecile said. "What happened?"

"It's Delphine's fault Vonetta's gone," Fern said.

Cecile turned to me. "Speak up, Delphine."

I didn't know what to say because it was true. It was easier to agree than to explain, so I said, "Yes. She left because of me."

My mother put her head down, cupping her forehead with one hand. It looked like she was praying but I knew she wasn't. I took a step toward her, then one away from her.

"I *told* you to look out for Vonetta." Her voice trembled like she was fighting herself. And then she spoke louder. "I told you but you don't listen!" She was up on her feet and Fern shrunk inside of herself. Shrunk into the ball I wanted to shrink into to protect myself. "You're hardheaded. You think you're grown and you know everything."

I stepped back, fearing the worst.

"And whose fault is that?" Big Ma was in the doorway, right behind me. "Who do you think you are, coming in here yelling at these children? I won't stand for it. You need to leave this house. Now!"

Big Ma was no match for my mother, but I knew she meant what she said.

Cecile seemed to grow bigger but she stood where she was. "I'll leave when my child is found and not a minute, hour, or day sooner." Cecile was the mountain. The crazy mother mountain. It was the calm in her voice that was crazy.

"Minute? I can get the sheriff up here in a minute," Big Ma said, while Fern said, "No, Big Ma. No, Big Ma."

Big Ma said, "This is my house. If I say you go, you're going."

"Get the sheriff," my mother said again, calm. Too calm. "I'm here for my child. I'll stay out there with the dog but I'm not going until I see my child."

Uncle Darnell was now in the room and stood between Big Ma and Cecile. Mr. Lucas tried to calm everyone down and then Ma Charles made her way into the room.

"This is my house. *My* house," Ma Charles said. She turned to Big Ma. "Ophelia Fern Charles Gaither, don't shame me."

My mother's face turned a shade darker when Ma Charles said all of Big Ma's names. In that moment, as I heard it myself for the first time, I knew it was partly true: My mother had left us eight years ago when my father said she had to name my baby sister Fern.

Big Ma turned to her mother. One minute she was puffed up with anger, and now she was just hurt. "You only see someone who gave you your bloodline." She meant us, my sisters and me. We were the bloodline. "But Ma, as sure as I'm standing here, she's been stirring up trouble and heartache from day one and I'm tired of it."

Ma Charles said, "She's a mother like you are. A mother can't rest until she knows her child is fed, safe, and well.

You can't be mad she's not here one minute, then mad she's here the next."

Big Ma just looked at her mother, wanting something from her, and then stomped off to her room. Uncle Darnell said, "Come talk to me, sis," and led my mother outside. And Miss Trotter said, "I tell you, I don't miss the picture shows or television at all. Not at all."

That left Fern and me alone. She on her bed and me by the door. I was used to my little sister running to me. There was this saying that my Muslim classmate, Rukia Marshall, had taught me: If the mountain won't come to Muhammad, then Muhammad must come to the mountain. As sure as Fern sat with her arms crossed, I knew she was the mountain and that it was my turn to come to her. I walked over and sat on the bed next to her. She uncrossed her arms and inched away, so I let her keep the distance.

"I was only looking out for you," I began.

"Well, don't, Delphine. I can look out for myself." She clunked her turtle head, a hard "Surely can." Fern was the baby I saw coming out of Cecile on the kitchen floor. She clung to me and hid behind me practically every day after that. I didn't believe Fern could look out for herself without me but I still said, "Okay." I had always seen myself as mighty and unmovable among my sisters. For the first time I felt so small next to my baby sister. Small like a hill. I added, "I'm sorry. I'm sorry about Vonetta."

She snapped, "Sorry doesn't bring Vonetta back."

"I know," I said softly. "I want her back here in this house. With us."

"You do not."

"That's not true, Fern. I miss her."

She turned her face to me, looking every bit like Cecile. "Pants on fire!" Even angry Fern stuck to Big Ma's rule about never using the word *liar*.

"I love Vonetta," I said, "but I don't always like her."

"You surely don't."

"And neither do you."

She said nothing.

"But she's our sister, and we want her back."

We sat on the bed until the space between us eventually closed.

Mississippi

Fern and I waited scrunched up into each other in the hallway like spies. It was the first time in too long a while that Fern let me near her. We could hear Cecile and Big Ma exchanging words. I mostly heard Cecile's voice. She wasn't screaming and acting crazy like I feared she would. When we heard her heavy footsteps, we ran out of the hall. As soon as Cecile passed to go to the bathroom, I went in to see that Big Ma was all right.

Big Ma was beating the yolkiness out of the few eggs our hens managed to lay. The hens hadn't been laying the same since the tornado, but today was the first day we collected nearly a dozen. Mr. Lucas said they'd be back to themselves once the chicken run and the nesting boxes were replaced.

I helped Big Ma make breakfast while she muttered angry words about my mother being in the house she was born in and how her own mother called Cecile "daughter" and took Cecile's side over hers.

I don't know how Uncle Darnell got my mother back in the house, talking to Big Ma, and then sitting at the table, but there she was, ready to eat and unbothered by Big Ma, who was still muttering and serving.

I brought out a pitcher of orange juice then took my place next to Fern, who sat practically under Cecile, and Cecile let her. Uncle D sat between Cecile and Ma Charles, and Ma Charles and Miss Trotter sat together and allowed no one between them at the table. Even when they fussed with each other, they fussed side by side. JimmyTrotter sat to my right, next to Mr. Lucas, who sat next to an empty seat that he patted each time Big Ma entered carrying a platter. Big Ma refused her seat next to him each time.

Finally, Big Ma stopped muttering and spoke her mind. "I won't sit at that table and I won't ask the Lord to bless it. No, sir. Surely won't."

"If you won't ask the Lord to bless it, I will," Ma Charles said. My great-grandmother, showing off for her sister and for my mother, said a short prayer for my mother for having made the journey, for Pa and Mrs. still traveling on the road, and for Vonetta—"Whatever His will, be done." Mr. Lucas was the first to "Amen" and Big Ma gave him a mean look, but he didn't take it back or give her a look of apology. Mr. Lucas waited for her to fill his plate.

My mother made no expression. I knew she was hungry and intended to eat no matter who cooked the food. All the while Uncle D called her "sis" and poked her and chatted away with her. It turned out that the Black Panthers at the People's Center had taken up a collection for Cecile to fly down here. Now she'd have to print flyers for them with her kitchen printer "from now until forever." But she shrugged like it was nothing, and my mother didn't like owing anyone anything.

Since Fern had so little on her plate, Big Ma came around with the meat platter and dropped a piece of ham and a strip of bacon before her. Fern lifted her turtle head and pushed the meat to the rim of her plate.

"Keep that up," Big Ma threatened.

"Fern don't eat meat," I told Cecile.

"Why's that?" Cecile asked Fern. "Your teeth hurting?"

Fern shook her head no. Then Cecile said, "Enough people in the world trying to silence us. Girl, you better speak up."

Both Ma Charles and Miss Trotter liked that and took turns mimicking Cecile's words.

Fern gave Cecile a look I didn't think she should give, but she did. She picked up her fork and tapped it against her plate. Tapped it in the same rhythm she would have banged her fists at her sides. Fern rested her fork and cleared her throat.

Wilbur's locked up in a pen.
Bambi's mother's roasting
Round and around and around
She goes
On whose plate
Nobody knows.
The people eat
Dead bacon meat
The people sing,
"We offed the pig,
We offed the pig."
The people eat and sing.

She bowed her head and said, "A poem by Afua."

Uncle Darnell and JimmyTrotter snapped their fingers. I followed and Cecile put her fork down for a second to snap fingers on both hands. Miss Trotter banged her fork against her plate and so did Ma Charles.

"Go on, Rickets," Ma Charles said. "You're nothing but bones, a big head, and big eyes, but you can sure say some words."

"Mighty tasty words," Miss Trotter added. "Hungry for some barbecue."

"You have a conscience," Cecile told Fern. "I don't have much of a conscience where food is concerned, especially when I'm hungry." She took the pieces of ham and bacon from Fern's plate. Cecile didn't eat pork as a rule, but gobbled the meat and looked to Uncle Darnell's plate for more. My mother wasn't Jewish or Muslim, like some of my friends at school, who didn't eat pork at all. Cecile was just hungry.

I tried not to stare at my mother but there was no corner of my eye that didn't see her. I thought I was beginning to know my mother, but I couldn't figure her out. I thought she would give Big Ma a crazy piece of her mind, but she let Big Ma say what she wanted to say, and she just sat there quietly, eating and looking for more food. I waited for something to happen. It was a relief that Miss Trotter was in a talkative mood.

"She surely does favor them," Miss Trotter said, studying my mother. "Favor all three."

"Surely does," Ma Charles said. "And strong, too! Tell 'em how far you walked, daughter," she said to my mother.

"Got a lift from the airport as far as the junction."

"Hear that? All the way from the junction," Ma Charles said, exaggerating her astonishment. She turned to Uncle Darnell. "What's that, son? Five, six miles?"

"About that," Uncle Darnell said.

"Strong, I tell you," Ma Charles said. "Where your people from, daughter?"

"That's not your daughter!" Big Ma said.

"Mama didn't mean—" Mr. Lucas started. But Big Ma said, "I don't care what she meant. I care what she says."

"Oh, hush," Ma Charles said.

If my mother was a little tickled it came out in her eyes but nowhere else on her face. She said, "Mississippi," with a forkful of food in her mouth without spitting out a bit. She finished chewing and swallowing and said, "My mother's people are from Mississippi. My father, St. Louis."

Both Ma Charles and Miss Trotter nodded, especially to the St. Louis part, like she had said, "Paris, France."

"She looks about Creek, like Papa's people," Miss Trotter said. JimmyTrotter gave me a wink. "Maybe Choctaw."

"She look more like my mother's people," Ma Charles said, which was her way of saying "plain old Negro."

"She ain't nothing to us," Big Ma said.

Cecile gave Big Ma—who seemed to want to fight—no reaction, although she seemed amused by Ma Charles and Miss Trotter each claiming her.

It was the first time I heard where my mother's family had come from. My sisters and I, we weren't just Trotters, Charleses, Gaithers, and Johnsons. We were pieces of other families we'd never know or see.

"Strong like my people," Ma Charles said. "Done give me these greats. All three of them."

And no one said anything. We were missing Vonetta.

Big Ma said, "Strong is sticking around. Raising 'em. Loving them. Not just dropping them like an animal in the woods."

I waited for it to come. Waited for the dark cloud. Waited for my mother to say the kind of thing that only

Cecile would say. I sat there afraid to swallow. But Cecile said nothing. Not one word.

"You're here, daughter," Ma Charles told my mother. "As sure as you're a mother I knew you'd come. I knew it." She said to Fern, "Rickets, go get my tambourine."

"No shaking that tambourine at the table," Big Ma said.

"Go on 'n get it, Rickets. You know where I keep it. Go on."

Fern went flying through the house in search of Ma Charles's tambourine.

Ma Charles said, "My Henry and I had pigs. A pen full. Remember, son?" Mr. Lucas yessed her. "Other folks left their families or jumped out the window during hard times. We had a horse for fertilizer, pigs, chickens, a garden, and the creek overflowed with fish. We didn't know a thing about starvation."

The um-hmms went around from Miss Trotter, Mr. Lucas, my uncle. Even my mother nodded.

"Oh, yes. We had pigs a-plenty, but someone left the pen open."

"Ma," Big Ma said.

Ma Charles went on telling her tale. "All them pigs gone, and it was a hungry winter."

"An unkind winter, as I remember it," Miss Trotter added.

"Not just for every Trotter and Charles, but for everyone

around here. We weren't the only ones depending on our small living." She said to Big Ma, "You got worse from me and then some when I finished with you. Might have been a hard winter, but what is a hog when you don't have your child?"

"Child, child, child," Miss Trotter said.

Fern returned with the tambourine.

Gone Crazy in Alabama

Although the house would never be the same, we made ourselves busy putting things in order. Uncle D and JimmyTrotter managed to rig up a clothesline, tying cords from the bent-but-planted pole to the remaining sturdy branch of the pecan tree. With more people under one roof, laundry day began early and clean sheets were a priority.

Mr. Lucas found parts of the wire chicken run two miles from the house, flattened and wrapped around some trees. He planned to get another one set up once he rebuilt the chicken coop. Sixteen hens were a lot of chickens to account for. They needed constant watching, and Fern and I had nowhere to go but the back and front porches. We brought the chickens up from out of the root cellar to get fresh air and sunlight. Fern did her best to keep the fussiest hens away from the cows, Butter especially.

Cecile stretched tall in the door frame and then stepped outside to join us on the back porch. I started to motion for Fern to be quiet. Cecile liked the quiet. It was one thing I remembered from being little and sitting with her in our house on Herkimer Street. The quiet kept her calm. She always closed the bedroom door on Vonetta and let her howl until she fell asleep. I raised my finger to my lips but there was no need to whisper "Shh." Fern ran off after a chicken headed for Mr. Lucas's land. Once Fern herded the lone chicken back to the flock, she stayed close to her chickens, her dog, and her cows. She'd look up to see that Cecile was there, but that was all.

Cecile's gaze roamed from the hanging sheets, up the broken pecan tree, to the animals, the garden, and then out beyond the pines until I was sure she was staring off into her mind. I knew better than to ruin it with chatter. As long as she let me be with her I kept the peace and quiet.

Shortly after one o'clock Caleb started to sing his song. I didn't have to puzzle over the meaning of the song. I got up and Fern and I ran around to the front. Cecile eventually followed.

I couldn't see the Wildcat but I knew it was coming. Two minutes feels like two hours when you're waiting. The tan-and-black car made its way up the road as far as it could before reaching the trees blocking its path. The Wildcat veered off the road and onto the field, bumping along toward the house. Fern shouted, "It's Papa!" and I felt sick all over again.

The Wildcat was here. Pa and Mrs. were here. My heart wanted to leap toward my father but my stomach soured. It was the first time in a long while that I feared my father. I dreaded the look of pain and disappointment I'd see in his eyes. I dreaded the words he had waiting for me. Without thinking about it I stepped closer to my mother until I felt her there. She stood firm, letting me stay.

Fern raced down to the car, and before I knew it the whole family was on the porch to greet them. I didn't move from my mother.

Pa got out of the car and came around and opened Mrs.'s door, giving her his hand. It seemed as if she didn't want to, but she eventually took it, and then she pulled herself up and out of the passenger seat. When she stepped out into full daylight, shielding her eyes, I could see that we were going to have a brother or sister. Not very soon, but the baby was more than a secret. The baby was real.

Fern threw herself over Pa. Instead of telling her she was too big for that, he held her tightly. She leaned over and kissed Mrs. and I felt Cecile's eyes on Fern kissing Mrs.'s belly.

"That's for my brother," Fern said.

"Could be a sister," Mrs. said.

Fern shook her head no. "Our good luck is gone," Fern said. "It's a brother."

If it weren't sad, it would have been funny. Mrs. hugged Fern to her belly and told her not to give up hope, and then Big Ma, Uncle Darnell, JimmyTrotter, Fern, and even Mr. Lucas surrounded them. Ma Charles and Miss Trotter stood on the front porch with Cecile and me.

It was both a happy and sad meeting. The hugs were more about Vonetta than about being glad to be among one another. And after that began to wind down my father and my stepmother moved toward us. Cecile and me. They were only a few feet away but their walk from there to here dragged on like the way time dragged on while I waited for the Wildcat to come into view. My father saw my mother first, and he led Mrs. toward us. My mother stepped forward and gave my father a kind of a smile but then went to shake Mrs.'s hand first.

"Congratulations," Cecile said to Mrs. "How are you feeling?" she asked plain and factual. Not sugary and phony.

For the first time that I had known her, Mrs. lied. She put on a face that wasn't her own and said, "I couldn't feel any better."

Miss Trotter said, "Why pay for a picture show when

you can stay home with family?" I wasn't sure she meant that in a nice way, but Ma Charles thought it was funny and the two cackled.

"We'd have been here sooner, but I had to stop every minute and a half to find a bathroom," Pa said.

Mrs. shot Pa a look and I knew all the honey and sweetness had flown out the window.

There was nowhere to hide. I faced my father. There was no running from him so I lifted my eyes and Pa said, "Come here, baby." He never called me "baby." The pain I'd been feeling began to melt, although it hadn't gone away completely. It couldn't. Not until Vonetta was home with us. I only knew at this moment, my father forgave me for not having done what I was supposed to do: look out for my sisters.

When Pa finally let me go, he cocked his head, looked Cecile up and down, and said, "I figured that's where they went."

Mrs. said, "Where what went?"

Pa let Mrs.'s question hang in the hot air. He looked at the pants my mother wore and shook his head. Cecile always wore men's pants. But then it dawned on me. My father didn't shake his head the way Big Ma did when she saw a woman wearing slacks. He shook his head because he recognized them. My mother had kept and been wearing his pants all these years. If he meant to jar my mother or make her smile, he failed. All he got was her everyday Cecile face.

* * *

It was a good thing Mr. Lucas had added the extra room to Ma Charles's house. Pa and Mrs. stayed on their side of the house while Cecile stayed on the other side, mostly with Uncle Darnell, who called her "sis" no matter how many times Big Ma said, "She's not your sister." Or Cecile was up under Ma Charles and Miss Trotter, who called her "daughter" or "dear one." Big Ma had eye rolls and "hmp"s for that as well.

That night Cecile didn't sleep out on the floor where Mr. Lucas, Uncle D, and JimmyTrotter slept. We pushed the twin beds together in our room and she slept between Fern and me. She cradled Fern while I held on to one of my mother's braids, and fell asleep twirling her braids for their coarse and soft feel. The smell of coconut oil. And she let me.

Caleb sounded the alarm early the next morning. Once JimmyTrotter said, "Sheriff Charles," we all gathered in the front room, but no one spoke. We waited as the black-and-white car barreled up to the house. He came alone. Without his dog. Without Vonetta. Big Ma lost her knees and melted down into the chair. Mr. Lucas, Pa, and Uncle Darnell rushed to her.

I studied the sheriff from the window. His hard, slow walk. The tilt of his hat. I studied him to know what he'd say before he said it. Cecile's hand squeezed my hand.

249

Tight. So tight I could scream. But I didn't.

JimmyTrotter opened the door and Sheriff Charles walked inside. He nodded once to cover greeting us all and said, "Folks," but he spoke only to Ma Charles thereafter. "Mama," he started.

"Speak, boy," Ma Charles said.

"Mama," he said again. "It was how I said."

Big Ma moaned and called for Jesus but Mr. Lucas was there.

"Taranada threwed her here and there. Li'l thing like that hardly stood a chance, but she's in the hospital. S'maritans found her. Picked her up. Took her to Mercy. One sore heinie, one broke arm. Face scratched up. Could have been worse."

And then the screaming and the hallelujahs broke out. JimmyTrotter, Fern, and I jumped and hollered and ring-danced. Sheriff shook his head and said, "Just like a bunch of . . ." He didn't say "Negroes." Everyone was too busy praising the Lord over Vonetta, and we refused to hear him.

Except for Mrs. "How dare you!" she said. "How dare you speak to this family like that!"

Pa said, "Calm down, dear. We're not in Brooklyn."

My mother said, "Call me what you want. I want to see my daughter."

Miss Trotter poked her sister and said, "Slim Jim Trotter and his two wives."

"Isn't it the truth?" the other said.

Darnell said, "Lou, you got the Wildcat. I'll take the truck."

A revived Big Ma said, "Let's all go see Vonetta!"

Mrs. was too disgusted to partake in the glee. She didn't understand; If you prayed for the miracle you'd sell your most treasured possession for, you don't care about anything else but waiting on that miracle. I knew I had a piece of the South in me but I didn't know it was that much.

Sheriff Charles said, "Now look. Mercy's a good Christian hospital but they don't want to see all you . . . Negroes showing up at once. I'll take the mother and father. Road's still not good."

We all wanted to go but Pa said, "Just me and Cecile." To the sheriff he said, "We'll take our car. I'll follow." Mrs. didn't like it but he said, "Marva, you're in a family way. You need to rest. We'll be right back."

Big Ma said, "Junior, I'm coming with you. I just have to get my hat and purse and change my clothes."

But Pa was already walking away. Sheriff Charles had a word with my father before he got in the patrol car. Pa called Cecile to come get in the car.

"Tell Vonetta we're glad she's not in the sweet by-and-by," Fern said.

"Tell Vonetta I'm sorry," I said.

Cecile said, "You'll tell her." But her voice was soft on

me and not pointed. I almost smiled. Then she slid into the front seat of the Wildcat. The Wildcat coughed a little before she started growling and rumbling. I stood on the porch and watched my mother and father follow the sheriff down the road.

Sad IRONS

Pa and Cecile had been gone for hours. All we could do was wait to hear more news about Vonetta. How she looked. Was she in casts and bandages? Was she conscious? When could she come home?

When I couldn't wait any longer, I did the one thing I was determined not to do. The one thing I dreaded since I knew we were headed south. I took the sheets off the clothesline and brought them inside for ironing.

Ma Charles's irons didn't have electric cords. They were her mother's irons. One was a wedding present to Ma Charles when she married Henry Charles, and the other she inherited when my great-great-grandmother Livonia passed away.

I sat each iron on the stove and turned on the flames. Instead of the canned spray starch that Mrs. preferred when she did iron, I made the starch in a bowl, the way Big Ma had taught me when we first drove down south. Water, Argo, and a bit of crushed lavender. I took the older iron and flicked a few drops on its surface. The drops hissed metal and lavender and evaporated almost instantly. The iron was ready. I dipped my fingers in the bowl, swirled them around, and flung the drops of starchy water onto the sheet laid out on the ironing board. There was nothing left to do but press hard.

I wasn't surprised to learn my great-aunt, like her sister, preferred her cotton sheets lightly starched and didn't trust the feel of permanent press fabric. Why should she be any different than her sister?

Both irons were small, but they were heavy and had their own way of being moved across the cotton fabric. I learned to handle both and pressed until sweat coated my forehead, neck, and arms. I pressed and I prayed. It was only right that pressing went with prayer. That and being sorry. Every wrinkle was a patch of sorry to be smoothed and flattened. I gripped the old wooden handle and pressed until the heat waned. Then I switched irons. If ironing stiff white cloth in the heat hadn't killed anyone who'd held the handles and pressed and prayed, then I could do what they'd done. I could iron until the cotton sheet was smooth.

Everyone had shown me what Big Ma called "a mercy" when I didn't deserve one. In my heart I knew I wouldn't have been so kind to Vonetta if her meanness had caused Fern to run off. I knew I would have made her feel worthless every minute that Fern was missing.

"Thought I smelled some oppression burning." Jimmy-Trotter snuck up on me. His oppression began with a long vowel "o." O-ppression. "White sheets?"

I could feel the smirk. There he was, grinning at me. Even that felt good because that was the JimmyTrotter I knew. "Yeah," I said.

"Don't let me stop you from oppressing."

"Very funny."

He bladed his finger across my forehead and flicked the sweat away. He wanted me to know how much I was sweating, as if I didn't know already.

He stood there for a while, I guessed to needle me some more. Then he said, "You're hard on Vonetta."

I set the iron on an unlit pilot to cool. "I know," I said.

"I had a brother. A twin."

"I know."

"I'd give anything . . ."

He couldn't finish. I whispered, "I know."

Sign of Love

The phone rang around seven. Two long rings. The shock of the first ring made everyone both jump and then freeze. Finally Uncle Darnell grabbed the phone and announced that it was Pa calling. He said, "Vonetta is well enough to come home as soon as they release her from the hospital."

We waited, excited to see Vonetta and to have her home.

All of the sheets were ironed and folded.

Big Ma and I cooked supper. Two chickens. Two heads of cabbage with corn relish. Rice. Potatoes. Rolls. Peach cobbler topped with pecans and sugar. Iced tea. Lemonade.

We waited.

We prayed and ate.

We waited some more.

Then Big Ma said, "We should have gone to the hospital. We should have gone to see about Vonetta."

"Her mama and papa are there to see about her," Ma Charles said. "That's all that's needed."

"Hmp. The way they ran out of here, those two . . ."

"You'd run too if it was your child."

"Hmp. Who was there when he couldn't pay for a doctor to birth them? Who was there to grow them up in all the right ways? Who? Who?"

Ma Charles wasn't moved by anything Big Ma said. "All of that is its own reward," she said. "No need to stand up and take a bow. Am I right, sister?"

"Right as the rain threatening to fall tomorrow."

But Mrs. looked worried with all of that talk about Cecile and Pa being gone long. She tried to be her "right on" Marva Hendrix self, but she looked like she was set adrift in a small boat without an oar, searching around for help. I hated to see her like that. I wanted the old Miss Marva Hendrix back.

"Mrs.," I said. "Can I make you some tea?"

She smiled closer to her real smile and said, "No, Delphine. I've drunk enough tea."

"Can I roll your hair for bed?" She used more than fifty sponge rollers to make her big curly Afro. When she hesitated I said, "I'll go get the rollers."

She was sitting up snoring before I finished rolling half

of her head. I looked down at her hands clasped on her small belly. The idea of having a new sister or brother became more real. Now that I knew Vonetta was alive and would be home any minute, I could enjoy the fact that there would soon be one more of us. I hoped that would be a good thing.

Mrs.'s head was a pink spongy globe. I led her to the back bedroom and then started to mop the kitchen floor. I had to be awake when Vonetta walked through the door. I had to tell her I was sorry.

I held out as long as I could but fell asleep, my arm propped against the windowsill. When the morning came, my neck was stiff and my elbows sore, but the Wildcat was in the gravel driveway, parked a little farther down from the house. My parents sat in the front seat talking. I almost yelled, "They're here! They're here!" But it was that they were parked away from the house that kept me from calling out. They didn't want us to know they were there, and for a moment I worried something was wrong with Vonetta.

But then they both finally got out of the car, and I stayed at the window wrapping myself in the sheer white curtains as I watched my mother and father. Watched how they were with each other. Watched how they were more than my parents. They were two people who knew each other. Liked each other. Even when all I could remember were the loud noises. The crash of things being thrown. The smell of fresh paint my father used to cover Cecile's writing on the wall. And yelling. More yelling. I was now seeing what I thought I'd never see. What I had long given up wishing for. I was seeing my mother and father together and not angry. All I wanted was a sign that we came from love. Now that I saw it, through this window, I didn't know what to make of it. How could it be that the more I saw of my parents, the less I knew them?

I watched them as they were fixed on getting Vonetta out of the backseat. Cecile squatted down at the back passenger seat and then emerged with Vonetta, who took a step or two before Cecile scooped her up. Pa tried to take Vonetta from Cecile but Cecile kept moving toward the house.

When they neared the porch, I couldn't contain myself. "They're here!" I shouted. "They're here! With Vonetta!"

Uncle Darnell had already left for school. JimmyTrotter was coaxing Sophie and checking on Butter, but I was sure he'd come running. Mr. Lucas jumped up and tried to look awake. Big Ma marched out from her room, probably with a thing or two on her mind. Ma Charles and Miss Trotter would soon be there.

I swung the door open and stepped aside to let them in. It was as if everything had turned around. Cecile didn't carry Vonetta around when she was a baby, but today she held Vonetta in her arms. Vonetta, who was far beyond

259

the age of being picked up, clung to Cecile like a shy child. Papa trailed in behind them.

Big Ma's arms were crossed underneath her breasts. "Where yawl been? Around the world and back?"

Cecile walked right past her and left that question to my father.

Pa took Vonetta from Cecile and laid her on the couch.

"VONETTA!" Fern was about to leap on her when JimmyTrotter grabbed her in midflight.

"Hold on, Fern. She broke some bones."

"Give her some room. Let her breathe," Cecile said.

I expected Vonetta to say, "Yeah. Let me breathe," or something like that. But she said nothing.

I knelt down so she wouldn't have to look up. "I'm so glad, Vonetta. I'm so glad you're here. I missed you," I said. "And I'm so, so sorry."

"Truly sorry," Fern said.

"Me too," Vonetta said shyly. Her face was covered in scabs, but I looked in her eyes and tried to hide the shock of seeing her face scratched up so badly. Vonetta didn't say anything else, but she lifted her arm to show me her cast.

All I could say was, "Wow," like a dummy. Fern asked if it hurt and Vonetta shook her head no and then yes.

I unbuckled my watch strap and said, "You can have my watch."

She shook her head no.

"All right. That's enough for now," Cecile said. "Give her some room. You all will be making your noise before you know it." She meant the way our voices followed one another's like a song. Our voices seemed to sing those songs less and less.

Everyone made a fuss over Vonetta, which was only right. Then Ma Charles asked, "What took you so long, son?"

"Speak up, Slim Jim Trotter," Miss Trotter said.

And Mrs. said to Pa, "Why didn't you call?"

My mother's face went to stone, which was about her normal face when she wasn't the crazy mother mountain. Ever since my mother walked inside my great-grandmother's house I had been bracing myself for her kind of crazy. I held my breath waiting for her to open her mighty mouth and say awful things, loud—laying it down, telling it like it is. But under all of this questioning, her face was expressionless but not hard or angry. She was focused on Vonetta.

Even though Cecile said to give Vonetta room, neither Fern nor I could leave her side. We clamored to see Vonetta, be with her, touch her. Her hair had been braided along both sides of her head in tight knots. I knew it was my mother's hand at work. I knew she braided Vonetta's hair and not some hospital nurse.

Fern kept touching Vonetta's crown, where the braid was fat and flat. "Don't," she said in her real voice. Even so, I was glad to hear it.

"I can loosen it for you," I said.

"No," she said. "No."

I expected Vonetta to be chatty. I expected her to perform everything from leaving the house, riding the bike, and getting thrown by the tornado and so on. But she said very little.

Pa said, "They let her lie there on one of them gurneys for nearly a day before anyone even looked at her. They took their time about treating her and finding her family and they took their time about signing her out. You know how that goes. Same old, same old."

Cecile didn't look at him once while he explained. She stuck to Vonetta.

"We should get this written up in the papers," Mrs. said. "They can't treat blacks this way."

"We'll do no such thing. Writing up a hospital. Who ever heard of that?" Big Ma said.

"From what I understand," Papa began, "she'd been thrown far. We're very lucky."

"Who needs luck when you have the good Lord," Ma Charles said.

"And it doesn't hurt that her great-great-grandpa could fly like a bird," Miss Trotter said.

"Oh, sister, stop telling those Indian tales."

"I'll stop when you stop telling your tales."

Big Ma told them both to stop fussing and to be thankful. But she was still angry at Pa for having been gone so long, and angrier at Cecile—who she called the "root of all evil." Fern and I waited for crazy to come out of our mother, but to our shock, Cecile behaved as if Big Ma wasn't there.

That night Mrs. was angry at Pa. Big Ma stayed angry at Pa and Cecile. I, for one, was glad I had seen my parents from the window and how they were together. I had to treasure it, because Pa and Cecile didn't look each other's way or say a word between them once we were all inside the house. No one seemed happier than Miss Trotter. She enjoyed the sounds of family—angry, miffy, joyful, and all else in between. At the table that night, with Pa and Mrs. on one side and Cecile, Vonetta, Fern, and I on the other, our family gave thanks that Vonetta was home safe. "If you call broken bones 'safe,'" Miss Trotter added, "then let us be grateful."

Uncle Darnell walked in with a gallon of cow's milk from the McDaniels' farm. Cecile said something to Vonetta, and Vonetta's head sank low. Uncle Darnell greeted everyone, said, "Hi, sis," to Cecile, and stood before Vonetta.

"You all right, Net-Net?" he asked.

Vonetta took one look at Uncle D and burst into tears. He just said, "It's all right, Net-Net. It's all right."

Kind of Truth

We had fallen asleep with both twin beds pushed together—Cecile, Vonetta with her cast, Fern, and I. Somewhere in the shifting to get a better sleeping position I felt my mother's absence. The space she left seemed extra-large. After so much warmth the bed was suddenly cool. I sprang up. Cecile had on her pants. My father's pants. She slung her drawstring bag over her shoulder and was leaving.

I followed her as she moved around carefully, without big, heavy footsteps. Cecile went through the kitchen to avoid everyone sleeping in the living room. She opened the back door and slipped outside.

"Go back, Delphine," she said.

"You're leaving? Where are you going?"

"Home," she said. "Oakland."

"But Vonetta's not better yet."

"She been found. There's a house full of y'all to take care of her."

"She wants you."

"She's got me. But I can't be here."

I thought she was talking about the South. That even though they had taken down the "White Only" signs, you still had to know your place. I thought that's what she meant.

I said, "It's not Oakland, I guess."

She said, "You got that right. It's not Oakland. Now, go back inside, Delphine."

"But why not let Uncle Darnell drive you?"

"I need to walk," Cecile said.

"There's Klan out there," I told her.

"There's Klan everywhere," Cecile said. "You just have to see them."

I knew she'd said something truthful and important, but that kind of truth wasn't on my mind. I said, "I'll worry you're out there in the night."

"You're twelve, Delphine. I'm grown. Go and be with your sisters. Lie down. Dream a dream. Say good-bye to anyone who'd care and thank everyone who was kind to me. Be good, Delphine. And take care of yourself. Take care of you."

She wrapped her arms around me, then kissed me on the top of my head, probably to let me know she was taller and that I had a ways to go before catching up. I watched her leave. And so did Caleb. This time he didn't sing his song, but he let out a whimper.

I knew my mother was grown but I couldn't let her go into the night, walking up the road like she was on the west side of Oakland. I went inside and found Uncle Darnell and Pa asleep next to each other, which meant Mrs. was sleeping with Big Ma in her room. I bent down and said, "Cecile left. She's walking down the road."

Pa turned over. "I'll get the Wildcat."

But Uncle Darnell sat up quickly and said a firm "No," like he was the older brother. "I'll get the truck. I'll take her and sit with her at the airport."

Pa started to say something, but Uncle Darnell said it again. "No, Lou. Stay here." And he was gone.

Act of God

I told my sisters Cecile had left. I said her plane left in the middle of the night and she had to catch it. They must have known I was spinning straw, but I didn't want them to think she left us like she had before, when I was four, Vonetta was two, and Fern wasn't even a month old. The house howled and cried for days. But that was mainly Vonetta filling the house with her yowling. Fern cried and cried, but I learned to put the bottle in her mouth and her baby doll next to her, even though she was too little to know she had a doll.

Wishing for Cecile to stay was as good as throwing a wish away on prayers that had been answered. We already had the impossible. Our mother had found her way to Ma

Charles's house in Alabama, even when the idea of her being here was as crazy as the thought of men hopping around like kangaroos on the *Goodnight, Moon*. And yet, she showed up. She was there for Vonetta, Fern, and me. It seemed wrong to cry over her leaving, even though it had never occurred to us that she would actually leave. This time we didn't howl and cry for days like when we were little. But we still cried.

Big Ma poked her head in our room to see what the sniffling was about and found us sobbing on the two beds pushed into one.

"Stop all that crying. We have a lot to be thankful for, starting with being under this roof Elijah Lucas rebuilt. Not everyone has their home standing and in living order, you know. Now go wash your faces and help me get things ready. Delphine, I need you to peel potatoes for hash browns and you're in here leading your sisters in the criers' choir. Come on. Come on, now."

And just like that, we got up and started moving. Just like we did when Big Ma had come to take over on Herkimer Street.

As much as I wanted to be seated and to enjoy my family, I was glad to have busy hands. The mention of cheese grits made Mrs. woozy but I just kept cooking and serving. And peeking at my family. Watching us all be together at the table. In fact, Fern gave thanks to Mr. Lucas for making our roof sturdy so we could all be underneath it.

Mr. Lucas said, "Ophelia, please sit down and enjoy this meal."

"Oh, no. So much to do," Big Ma said.

Then Mr. Lucas said, "Woman, I said, sit down."

The surprised and jokey sounds that sprang up from everyone but Mrs. were enough to bring the house down. Then Ma Charles shook her tambourine to be heard and the room quieted.

"Listen here, son," she told Mr. Lucas, who was instantly cowed. "Only two people can tell this woman what to do: her ma and her husband. Unless you're her husband you can't tell her a thing."

Mrs. gasped in horror. "This isn't 1869." She had more to say but Pa took her hand and Miss Trotter said, "Hush, young'n."

Big Ma might have been embarrassed—I wasn't sure— and fled into the kitchen. Then Mr. Lucas stood up like he was going after her.

Ma Charles said to Mr. Lucas, "Son, you stay with us. Eat with us. Sleep on this sofa until your house is built up. Heaven knows we were saved from that tornado by an act of God, and that you've built our house up strong over the years."

Mr. Lucas didn't move. He knew to wait for the other shoe to drop. "Yes, Ma."

"But as long as I have an unmarried daughter under this very roof you rebuilt, your place is out here with the rest of us. When you're married you can always go in the kitchen or down the hall to see about your wife."

Mr. Lucas sat down.

Between my sisters and me "oohing," our father, uncle, and cousin slapping hands, and Miss Trotter cackling, the house was lit up with laughter. I couldn't believe my ears. My great-grandma told the man who'd rebuilt her house that he had to marry my grandmother. I took the gravy bowl back into the kitchen, where I found Big Ma fluttering and grinning. She shooed me out of the kitchen and said she'd be there with more gravy.

Just as I returned to my chair, Mr. Lucas told my great-grandmother, "I'll go to the courthouse in the morning, Ma."

Mrs. seemed outraged and confused by the whole thing. She stood up. "But no one asked Mother Gaither what she—" and Ma Charles said nicely, "You hush up, little missus, and take care of what's cooking in your pot. Get off your feet and hush up."

My father said to Mr. Lucas, "Can't just show up to the courthouse without a bride."

Mrs. still didn't like any of it and refused to eat in a house full of "wrong-thinking people with male-chauvinist-pig ideas." Miss Trotter clapped her hands at all of that chauvinism talk. She thought those words were just grand. Pa put his finger to his lips instead of outright telling Mrs. to hush like Ma Charles did.

When the hoopla died down a bit, Mr. Lucas said to my father, "You're right about that, son. Can't go to the courthouse without a bride."

Finally Big Ma came out of the kitchen with a full gravy boat. Mr. Lucas stood up, cleared his throat, and said to Big Ma, "Ophelia Gaither . . ."

Her mother said, "Charles. She's a Charles."

Her aunt said, "And by blood, a Trotter."

Fern said, "And a Fern!"

Mr. Lucas shook his head at the ordeal, took in a big breath, and exhaled before trying again. "Ophelia Fern Charles Gaither from the Trotters, will you come with me to the courthouse and sign some papers?"

Big Ma said, "I don't know why we have to make a grand Negro spectacle out of everything. I'll get my hat."

Miss Trotter said, "The courthouse!" showing all her teeth. "Hear that, sister? Legal."

"Under God, sister. Godly," the other said.

Maypop and Dandelion

Big Ma and Mr. Lucas returned with their courthouse papers, only to find Vonetta and Fern practicing their walk down a make-believe church aisle in the living room. Vonetta looked more like Frankenstein than a flower girl, limping and lugging her white-casted arm while Fern imitated her so there would be two Frankenstein flower girls. Both had missed out on being Pa and Mrs.'s flower girls. No one would deny them their only chance.

I expected Big Ma to put an end to Vonetta and Fern's traipsing and prancing but she said she was tired and needed to sit down.

Ma Charles and Miss Trotter put their heads together to speculate about what Big Ma meant by "tired," and if she would go through with the wedding vows. Mrs. said she had the right to change her mind. Although each thought there was a chance that she might not go through with it, both sisters said, "Hush," and went on speculating.

I'd made a gallon of iced tea earlier and brought out four full glasses. Two for the Trotter sisters and one for Mrs. Everyone else could get their own. I took the fourth glass down the hall and knocked before pushing open the cracked door to Big Ma's room. She sat by the nightstand, her hat still on her head, its feather drooping, and her black Bible in her lap. A single sheet of paper lay facedown on the Bible. Big Ma caressed the paper along its center crease like it was a living thing that needed caressing. Her eyes were lost in the nothingness of the wallpaper lilies.

My first guess was that Miss Trotter and Ma Charles were right about Big Ma. She was having second thoughts about marrying Mr. Lucas. I spoke softly so as not to startle her. "Big Ma, do you want me to put that away? It looks important." I pointed to the paper.

Her hand brushed across it. "I almost forgot it," she said, as if she was talking to air. "I almost forgot it. Then I remembered, you have to bring the death . . . bring the . . ."

By its coloring and its less than sharp crease, I knew it was something Big Ma had been keeping for years. Something she had gotten into the habit of rubbing, like she was doing now.

It wasn't the courthouse papers from her trip into town with Mr. Lucas. It was my grandfather's death certificate.

She looked up as if she was seeing me for the first time. "Just let me sit for a minute, Delphine."

I placed the coaster with the glass of iced tea on the nightstand. She didn't look like she would move, so I removed the long, dull-ended pin from her hat and lifted the sea-green hat from her hair, her own hair, and returned her Sunday hat to its eight-sided box. I unbuckled her shoes, pulled off each one, and rubbed the swelling in both feet. Then I left her alone.

A week later, Pastor Curtis came to the house with an even bigger Bible than Big Ma's black Bible and married our grandmother to her next-door neighbor in the living room. Pa and Uncle Darnell insisted on standing on both sides of Big Ma to walk her up to Mr. Lucas and the pastor while she fussed about being escorted like a common criminal. Instead of pronouncing all of Big Ma's names, the pastor presented them as "Mr. and Mrs. Elijah Lucas." Ma Charles raised her tambourine as high as she could and gave it a good shake. Vonetta and Fern threw purple maypop petals and blew dandelions as they hobbled down the aisle. Since Vonetta hobbled, Fern also hobbled. Miss Trotter scolded them for using "good medicinals" to throw at the rug. Big Ma told Vonetta and Fern to clean up every last bit of field weed and seed before they went to bed. Mrs. behaved herself, although I caught her shaking her head woefully when the pastor called Big Ma Mrs. Elijah Lucas and not Ophelia Lucas.

In spite of Big Ma's fussing, I knew my grandmother was happy, but no one grinned wider than Mr. Lucas. Like Ma Charles said, "He waited longer than Jacob waited for Rachel."

Miss Trotter said, "I call that waiting, sister. I surely do."

SoutheRN Good-bye

Ma Charles and Miss Trotter were full of "what-to-dos" for Mrs. and the baby. Mrs. started looking for Pa to save her from their home remedies.

"Are you sure you can't stay another couple of days?" JimmyTrotter asked. "Butter's about to drop her calf any day now. Could even be tonight."

"Sorry, son," my father said. "They won't hold my job forever."

JimmyTrotter said to me, "Wish you could be here with me when I pull out this calf. I got a good feeling."

"I'm a Brooklyn girl," I told my cousin. "I don't go around pulling out calves, JT."

He threw one arm around my neck, dragged me near,

and pressed his knuckle into my forehead.

Fern stopped dead in her tracks. "What do you mean, pull out a calf?"

"How do you think that calf is going to get out of her?" Vonetta said. Although her "heinie" still hurt when she walked, Vonetta was coming back to her old self, and we were treating her like her old self. Not entirely, but close enough.

"All right, young lady." Mrs. wagged her finger at Vonetta. I was tired of scolding my sister and was glad Mrs. stepped in. "Honey," Mrs. said to Pa. "All this talk about pulling out baby cows is making me dizzy. Let's get in the car and on the road."

When Fern was out of earshot I asked my cousin, "What about Sophie?"

"We'll try her out one more time. Get her with a calf. See how it goes." He shrugged but there was nothing hopeful in his voice.

I took JimmyTrotter aside and said, "Fern is right. Maybe you milking her isn't enough. Maybe she needs her calf to get her milk and then she'll give more. Have you thought of that?"

He slugged me. Light. "Get in the car, Brooklyn."

"I'm getting, JT. I'm getting. Just think about it," I said, although I wasn't yet finished with my hugs.

He gave me another noogie sandwich, to let me know that he could, and somewhere in that we hugged a real hug.

Between Mr. and Mrs. Lucas, the Trotter sisters, cousin JT, and Uncle D, we must have made at least three rounds of hugs, "Yawl be careful," and "See you real soon," with the Lord's blessing added for good measure. Mrs. called it the "Southern good-bye" because it went on and on and on and there was nothing like it in New York. "People just aren't that way," she said.

Uncle Darnell and Pa shook hands, and Uncle D gave Mrs. a hug, and then he hugged each one of us. During my last round of hugs with my uncle, he patted his pockets and said, "Delphine. Almost forgot." He held out a folded paper napkin. "From Sis." He saved his favorite, Net-Net, for last and whispered something in her ear. She whispered back.

"All right, drive safely, family." And then he was in the truck he shared with Mr. Lucas, his stepfather, and off to work.

And finally we did the last part of the Southern good-bye. We were all in the car and Mr. Lucas called out, "Drive careful."

Big Ma said, "Don't make a fuss over everything. Every good-bye isn't gone."

Butter mooed something awful and everyone laughed.

"Well, you better get gone," Ma Charles told us. "The cow said it all."

"If you call that gone," Miss Trotter said.

Fern mooed and Vonetta said, "Cut it out."

Then Caleb got in on the good-byes and sang his dog song. We heard him singing when we could no longer see the house. And all I could think was how strange it would be to leave all of this. Cows, chickens, the creek. All of it. And yet part of me was ready to go home.

Vonetta lifted her cast to point to the napkin in my hand. "What is it?" Vonetta asked.

"Yeah, what?"

I unfolded it and let it fall in my lap. "A letter. From Cecile."

"Where's mine?" Vonetta asked. "I'm the one who was nearly killed."

I'd be hearing that for a long time. "I'll share it," I said, even though I didn't want to. I wanted to take my letter to a secret place and enjoy my mother's words, even if she'd written *You're hardheaded, Delphine*, like I knew she could. No matter what Cecile wrote, no matter how short or how mean, I planned to read it alone, over and over, to try to learn who my mother was.

I cleared my throat in dramatic Vonetta fashion, hoping to get a smile out of her. Then I read.

Dear Delphine,

    A woman who kicks up dust to make her path can walk through a storm. If her child can walk through a storm then she can. She can walk through the violent wind with peace inside her. She does not walk for herself.

She is not there for herself. She is not there for her anger.
She is not there for her own pain. She is there for her
child. She can withstand it all. Even if she leaves without
the child in her arms, she carries the child with her. All of
her children. With her. In her. The storm cannot take her
peace away. A storm cannot take the child away.

Your Mother.
Cecile

P.S. Things do fall apart.
P.P.S. But you're strong enough to walk through the
storm.
P.P.P.S. (if there is such a thing): Walk on, daughter.
Walk on.

"You see!" Vonetta cried. "Her poem is about me."

Mrs. made a "hmp" sound. And I thought it was funny that she sounded like Big Ma.

"I'll tell you one thing," Mrs. said to Pa. "When we get home, you're going to trade in this tin can on wheels for a brand-new car. That's the end of this Wildcat."

"Oh, is that so?" Papa said.

"You think I'm joking. I want this old car gone."

Whatever Mrs. was mad about she took out on Pa's faithful old girl, the Buick Wildcat. Although Pa's voice teased, I knew Mrs. meant what she said.

Keeps on Ticking

I believe Mrs. truly hurt the Wildcat's feelings. Once Pa parked the car on Herkimer Street, he couldn't get the car to growl, let alone purr. She sat there, dusty from nine hundred miles of driving, and refused to move another inch.

We were so used to her growling and rumbling, announcing our father's comings and goings. I couldn't remember not having her. We had been warmed and comforted by the rumbling of the Wildcat as we drove off to wherever Pa was taking us. We made up car-riding games for extra-long trips. We'd sung along with any group or singer who joined us through speakers as the bass boomed low and the treble pined high. We had some good times in the Wildcat. It was hard to see her go.

Pa was determined to save his precious car. His old girl. It didn't matter how many hours he spent with the hood up and his hands scarred up and blackened with oil. The Wildcat refused to turn over.

Vonetta, Fern, and I sat on the stoop and watched the tow truck come and take Papa's Wildcat away.

"At least we made it back to Brooklyn," I said.

Vonetta nodded. "She could have conked out on the road in the middle of the night."

"And we'd have to hitchhike all the way home."

For a second, I thought Vonetta would burst out into a chorus of "Hitch Hike," and we'd be her Marvin Gaye backup singers doing the "Hitch Hike" dance. But since Vonetta didn't sing a note or make a move, I let it go.

We agreed it was best they took the car away while Pa was at work. I didn't think he'd want to see it being hooked up to the big monster truck and dragged away. It was hard enough to watch it ourselves.

We were home for a few days and already bored. It wasn't as if we'd had a lot to do down in Alabama, but being down there was nothing like being in Brooklyn. We missed our chickens, and cows, our dog, and endless pecans. We missed hiking through the pines and wading in the shallow end of the creek. We sulked long enough about good times in Papa's car. But we missed Uncle D and Big Ma. And JT and the Trotter sisters. We missed the fun and the fussing. And when we really got bored we compared our bug bites and scars, probably just to remember we had been down in Alabama.

When there seemed to be nothing else to say, Vonetta asked Fern, "What time is it?"

I looked down at my Timex. "It's —"

"Not you, Delphine." She turned to Fern. "What time is it?"

I wanted to pop Vonetta in the head. She was still wearing the braids Cecile made and they were beginning to unravel, but she wouldn't let anyone touch her head. That didn't stop Mrs. from commenting about Vonetta's strands sticking out. Vonetta only pretended she didn't hear her.

I kept thinking about my mother and what she wrote to me. If Cecile could keep her craziness inside of her and walk into a place where she wasn't welcomed by everyone, and see Pa with the woman he married and their baby on the way, then I could keep a lid on it where Vonetta was concerned. I could try a little harder. But honestly, Vonetta didn't make it easy.

Fern looped the watch around her arm so the face sat on her wrist instead of dangling downward, like usual. It was a wonder she managed to keep that watch on her puny wrist. But she did.

"It's ten minutes past two o'clock."

"That's not how you say it," Vonetta snapped. "When you get to third grade, say, 'It's two ten.' Then everyone

283

will know you've been telling time for a while."

I hadn't expected that from Vonetta. She'd said something useful to Fern. Something to make the third grade easier. Like a big sister would.

"I'll show you other time-telling tricks. Like the 'by fives' and 'the tos.' You'll need to know those."

"By fives and twos?"

"Yeah. Five *to* three. Get it? Five minutes to three. There's so many ways to tell the time but you don't want to do it the baby way. Go ahead. Ask me what time it is."

"But you don't have a watch."

Vonetta huffed and puffed and I wanted to say something but I kept my mouth shut and tried to walk through the storm.

"Just ask me what time it is."

"What time is it, Vonetta?" we both asked.

I expected Vonetta to snap, "Not you, Delphine," but she didn't. She said, "It's time to get my watch back o'clock."

Fern and I cheered! We cheered and Vonetta said, "Let's not make a federal case out of it." Then she paused. "Just come with me."

"You know where she lives?" I asked.

"Yeah," Vonetta said. "Let's go. But *I* knock on the door, Delphine. Not you."

I shrugged to not make a big deal of it and then let Vonetta lead the way. I was supposed to tell her something useful, like a big sister would, like, "If you could make it

through a tornado, you can make it through anything."
She already seemed to know that. And sometimes it was
better to just hush. This was one of those times.

What a sight we made. Vonetta's limp wasn't so bad,
but she still had her cast in a sling. Fern skipped some
and walked some and kept saying the words to the Timex
commercial but in her own rhythm: "It takes a licking and
it keeps on ticking."

I did what my sister asked. I let her go to the door while
I stayed back. But I was there. That was all my sisters
needed to know. I'd be there. Always.

Author's Note

I couldn't think of a better way to say good-bye to the
Gaither family than to tell their family history, especially
when it seems the family is falling apart. Like most African-Americans, the Gaithers' African roots are entwined
with European ethnicity. While it is common for some
African-Americans to claim Native American ancestry
with little to substantiate their claims, it is also true that
African-Americans and Native Americans from the southeastern and northeastern parts of the US have a complex
and shared history. Who better to tell both sides of this
story than the elder Trotter sisters, both having one-
quarter Creek blood and being descendants of Creek
freedmen?

As described in the story from one elder's account,

some southeastern Native American nations partici-
pated in the sale and ownership of slaves. It is also true
that some African-American freedmen—former slaves—
lived separately as freedmen among the "Five Civilized
Tribes" (the Cherokee, Chickasaw, Choctaw, Creek, and
Seminole Nations), while some also married within the
nations and had blood descendants. Many freedmen and
native-owned slaves marched west with their host Native
American tribe in the early 1830s, when Native Americans
from the southeastern states were forced to remove themselves from their land in the inhumane journey known
as the Trail of Tears. In the Treaty of 1866, the freedmen
were granted full tribal status and rights, although their
status and benefits continues to be challenged today. For
more information, I recommend *Black Indians: A Hidden
Heritage* by William Loren Katz and *Africans in America:
America's Journey through Slavery* by Charles Johnson,
Patricia Smith, and the WGBH Series Research Team.

With so much happening in 1969, I turned to my diaries
to remember what was important to me as a tween back
then. On July 20 I wrote, "The astronauts landed and set
foot on the moon," and months later on October 18 I wrote
"Jackson Five!" after watching them for the first time on
The Hollywood Palace, a variety show that aired on ABC.
To tell the story of the Gaither sisters, particularly with
Vonetta's coming to terms with her uncle, I exercised liter-
ary license by moving the date that the sisters would have
known about the Jackson Five. Vonetta's pain, however, is

real. To learn more about the Apollo moon missions, I recommend *Team Moon* by Catherine Thimmesh and *Mission Control, This Is Apollo* by Andrew Chaikin and astronaut Alan Bean. I also recommend YouTube to see videos of the Apollo 11 launch and moon landing, as well as the debut of the Jackson Five on *The Hollywood Palace*.

If Delphine and her family seem real to you, it is because the *idea* of them is real. The Trotters, Charleses, Gaithers, and Johnsons tell an American story in their crossings, struggles, and strides, and in their witnessing of and taking part in history. We need not look further than our own families to find unique histories that touch upon and comprise American history. It was an honor and my pleasure to tell their family story to you.

I thank my HarperCollins family for supporting my need to tell stories that include known and little-known histories. I couldn't have had a truer advocate for these stories and a fiercer caretaker of this family than my editor, Rosemary Brosnan. I also thank my colleague and dear friend Leda Schubert, who has great instincts. Thank you to my Facebook friends, who responded eagerly and creatively to my query for Big Ma's name, especially to Stephen Bramucci, Janet Fox, Jim Hill, Sheryl Scarborough, and Nicole Valentine, who got it right. I thank those who've shared their accounts of their mixed ancestry, both documented and undocumented. Most of all, I thank my readers, who've come to know and love Delphine, Vonetta, and Fern—and every Gaither, Charles, Trotter, and Johnson.

Augustus Trotter Descendants

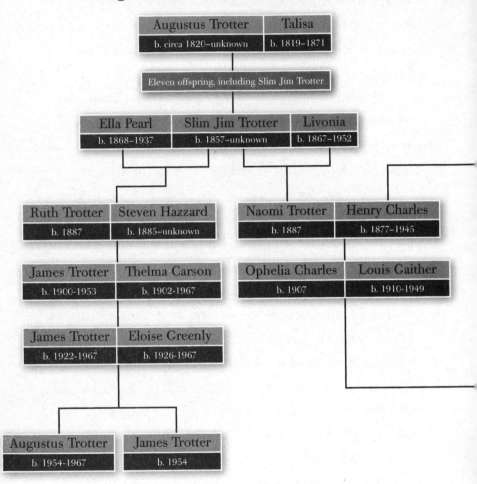

Augustus Trotter | **Talisa**
b. circa 1820–unknown | b. 1819–1871

Eleven offspring, including Slim Jim Trotter

Ella Pearl | **Slim Jim Trotter** | **Livonia**
b. 1868–1937 | b. 1857–unknown | b. 1867–1952

Ruth Trotter | **Steven Hazzard**
b. 1887 | b. 1885–unknown

Naomi Trotter | **Henry Charles**
b. 1887 | b. 1877–1945

James Trotter | **Thelma Carson**
b. 1900-1953 | b. 1902-1967

Ophelia Charles | **Louis Gaither**
b. 1907 | b. 1910-1949

James Trotter | **Eloise Greenly**
b. 1922-1967 | b. 1926-1967

Augustus Trotter | **James Trotter**
b. 1954-1967 | b. 1954

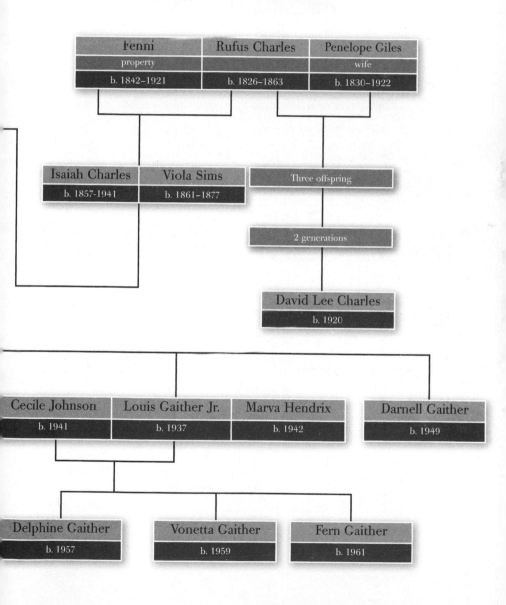

About the Author

Rita Williams-Garcia's Newbery Honor–winning novel, *One Crazy Summer*, was a winner of the Coretta Scott King Author Award, a National Book Award finalist, the recipient of the Scott O'Dell Award for Historical Fiction, and a *New York Times* bestseller. The sequel, *P.S. Be Eleven*, was also a Coretta Scott King Author Award winner and an ALA Notable Children's Book for Middle Readers. She is also the author of six distinguished novels for young adults: *Jumped*, a National Book Award finalist; *No Laughter Here, Every Time a Rainbow Dies* (a *Publishers Weekly* Best Children's Book), *Fast Talk on a Slow Track* (all ALA Best Books for Young Adults); *Blue Tights*; and *Like Sisters on the Homefront*, a Coretta Scott King Honor Book. Rita Williams-Garcia lives in Jamaica, New York, is on the faculty at the Vermont College of Fine Arts in the Writing for Children & Young Adults Program, and has two adult daughters, Stephanie and Michelle, and a son-in-law, Adam. You can visit her online at www.ritawg.com.

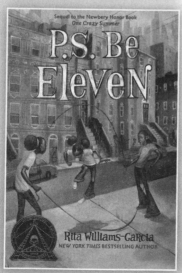